WHEN I FALL IN LOVE

by Cora Lee

Editing by Jude Simms.

Cover by Erin Dameron-Hill at EDH Professionals.

ISBN 978-1-944477-32-5

Published in the United States by More Than Words Press

Chapter 1

Kent, August 1816

SYLVIE DEVEREAUX SAT IN HER usual place on the brown sofa, lightly rubbing the worn spot on the arm. Her grandparents occupied the wooden chairs on either side of the fireplace, where a small fire burned to try to combat the unusual chill. The low, red light of the evening sun filtering through the windows wasn't quite bright enough to see by anymore, so Sylvie lit the oil lamp on the table beside her, hoping to get some mending done before she went to bed.

Her fingers lingered on the lamp a moment, the smooth metal cool to the touch for a few moments before it began to warm. This particular lamp had been a rather costly wedding gift to her grandparents from both their families, the result of a numerous relatives pooling what they could spare to purchase something truly beautiful...and useful. Sylvie's grandparents had brought it with them when they emigrated from France, a symbol of the family they left behind and the hope they cherished for their future.

Was this the future they had envisioned?

"How does the field look, Grandpère?"

It was a topic they had discussed at least once each day during the growing season, usually in this fashion around the fireplace or while they ate supper, for as long as Sylvie could remember. Grandpère would inevitably talk about the height of the wheat, the color and strength of the stalks, or a myriad of other tiny but important details that signaled the health of their crop.

But this season had been different. This *weather* had been different.

His silence stretched out so long that Sylvie put down her needle and looked up at her grandfather. His eyes had met his wife's, his mouth turned down into a hard frown that didn't ease when he finally answered.

"Not good, ma chérie. We may not have much of a crop this year."

Not a surprise and yet wholly surprising all at the same time. Sylvie had been half-expecting this bit of news for the past several weeks now, but to hear her grandfather say it aloud was like a physical blow to her chest.

"Still too wet," her grandmother added, returning to her own sewing. "The kitchen garden has been struggling all summer, too."

Sylvie had noted the lack of production in the kitchen garden herself, trying to find enough produce to eat with each meal.

There was never enough, and what was growing was undersized and slow to ripen.

Grandpère nodded. "And too cold. Wheat doesn't like a great deal of heat, but it needs some warmth."

"And sun." Sylvie pressed her lips together, recalling the abnormally high number of dark, rainy days they'd had this year. Even this day they'd only seen a bit of sun as it set, and that was more than most. "Do you think we'll be able to pay rent this quarter?"

The fire gave a loud pop and sent out a plume of thick smoke as he sighed heavily. "For the first time since you were a little girl, I don't know. If we get enough sun in the next few weeks, there may be something to harvest. But if the rain keeps falling..."

He didn't have to finish his sentence. If the rain kept falling, any wheat that had managed to grow in their field despite the conditions would rot at the root and there would be no harvest. Sylvie also didn't need to ask if he'd thought of borrowing money —her parents might have a little to spare, but likely not enough to cover rent for the farm. And they were in France with no way to send money or to return to England themselves. A bank loan might be a possibility, but without a crop to use as assurance…

"Try not to worry," Grandmère said, turning in her chair to meet Sylvie's gaze, her face partially cloaked in shadows. "There is still time to figure something out."

There was a measure of comfort in her words, but Sylvie was too practical to be swayed very much by them. If Grandpère said things were looking dismal, then there was reason to worry.

"There are always my animals."

In addition to the three people and the wheat fields, the farm housed a flock of geese, a few goats, some laying hens, and a dairy cow, all of whom would need to be fed through the winter. They weren't truly hers, but Sylvie had taken over caring for the farm's livestock as an adolescent and had hand raised many of the goats and geese herself. As a result, Grandpère had taken to calling them hers.

He raised a hand to object, but she held up her own to stop him. "Not Moses, of course." She suppressed a shudder at the thought of sending her special pet, a goose that she'd raised from an abandoned egg, off to someone's dinner table. "But the others should fetch a good price. That is why we keep them, and if it means keeping our home..."

Grandmère sent her a sympathetic look, then sighed herself. "Hopefully it won't come to that."

"But if we need to," Sylvie continued, turning their alternatives over in her mind, "it wouldn't be that different from other years. We've sold animals before."

"Yes, when we run out of room for them," Grandpère answered gruffly. "I will go to London and talk to his lordship myself before we sell off your entire collection."

Sylvie was certain Grandpère wouldn't even know what their landlord, the Marquess of Whitby, looked like, let alone find the wherewithal to go and speak to the man, but she kept that to herself. She also noted the red creeping into Grandpère's cheeks that couldn't all be attributed to the fire and turned the conversation to a new topic. "Perhaps I can take in some mending, then, or do some cooking for the neighbors. Mr. Mathison next door is a bachelor, and so is Mr. Ross across the way—I could speak to them both tomorrow."

Grandpère nodded, his face returning to its normal color. "I suppose it wouldn't hurt to inquire. And if we do end up with enough wheat to pay the rent, you'll have a little money put by for your future."

Her future. Sylvie suppressed a shiver and tried to focus on her needle going in and out of the soft, worn fabric of her second best dress. When Grandpère died, her father would likely be allowed to take over the copyhold on the farm if he chose to, but there was no telling when he and her mother would return, or if they'd even want to take up farming again. What if they decided to stay in France? They had a comfortable home there now with her mother's parents. What was there to come back to here except unending hard work and rain?

Sylvie gave up on her mending and said goodnight to her grandparents, trudging slowly up the stairs to the bedchamber she'd occupied all her life. How much longer would it be hers?

What would she do when it wasn't?

Cold water dripped onto Kit Mathison's face, which was occasionally accompanied by a chilly breeze. He blinked his eyes open but quickly squeezed them shut again, pulling the blanket up over his face to block out the small deluge. But instead of soft, dry blanket, he was met with sopping fabric that threatened to drown him before he could rise from his bed.

"Thomas, you've left the tent flap open again," he said with a yawn, his eyes still tightly shut to keep the water out of them. "It must have rained last night."

He felt about for a patch of dry cloth to wipe his face with and found part of his nightshirt that was unaffected. Rolling over onto his side, he pushed the blanket off and struggled to a sitting position as the dripping continued to wet his hair and clothes. "Thomas?"

Kit opened his eyes to find that he was not, in fact, in a tent behind the house with his younger brother, as his sleep-addled mind had believed, but alone in the big bed in the master's chamber.

"What the devil is going on?"

Another cold stream landed in his lap and he leaped out of bed. What the devil *was* going on? He held his hands out, palms up, eyes wide as he looked around the room.

Yes, it was definitely raining inside the house.

His house.

And there was a very large hole in *his* roof.

He stood in the corner of the room for a moment, unmoving except to blink, staring dumbly at the raindrops falling through the ceiling. How did this happen?

How much would it cost to repair?

Kit shook himself and set about dressing in dry clothes, thankful that the rain hadn't damaged his wardrobe...yet. He made his way down the stairs and stopped in the kitchen to butter a piece of bread, shifting the bread from one hand to the other as he put on his old, patched tailcoat and hat.

"All right, let's see how bad it is."

The rain had abated and the bread was reduced to crumbs by the time Kit stepped out the front door. He managed to wrestle the tall ladder and a large tarpaulin out of the barn with the help of one of the stable lads and hauled them one at a time to the house. When the two of them had propped the ladder against the house as close as they could to Kit's bedchamber, Kit climbed resolutely to the top with a rope tied to the tarpaulin while the stable lad held the bottom of the ladder steady. The ladder was just tall enough to reach the second story of the house, forcing Kit to scramble up onto the roof to survey the damage.

"How does it look?" the stable lad called?

Kit stayed low, crawling from the edge of the roof toward the hole, his eyes growing wider as he drew nearer.

"Oh no."

A large portion of the roof had collapsed into the attic space some time ago, judging by the weathering of the timbers poking out. And each time rain fell from the sky during this very wet summer, it had collected in the newly bared attic—

he could see the water stains on the attic floor—weakening the structure.

The rain that morning was merely falling through a ceiling that had been rotting away for weeks.

Kit sighed wearily. "How could I have missed this?"

He spent a few more minutes surveying the damage, then pulled the tarpaulin up to the roof and secured it over the gaping hole, trying to commit the details of the damage to memory so he could make a sketch later. A careful check of the other parts of the roof he could reach yielded even more information—three other places where shingles were loose or damaged, and water was likely already getting in.

When Kit reached the ground again, his stable lad wasn't the only one waiting for him.

"Moses! Have you come to swim in my bedchamber?"

The big white bird looked up at Kit and turned sideways, asking to be scratched the way Kit's childhood dog had done once upon a time. Both Kit and the stable lad obliged before hefting the ladder once again and hauling it back to the barn, with Moses waddling alongside them.

Once the ladder was stowed, the stable lad went back to his usual work and Kit headed back to the house, walking slowly around the perimeter looking for other issues.

"The roof was damaged, you see," Kit explained to the goose as they circled the house, "and I didn't realize it until just today. It's made a terrible mess inside the house, and I fear it's going to take a long time to restore."

A gust of wind blew through, ruffling Moses's feathers. He resettled his wings with a little shake.

"Indeed."

With another sigh, Kit made note of a couple of places under the eaves that were showing early signs of water damage. "Do you want to come in while I write these all down? Or shall I walk you home first?"

The first few times Kit had met Moses, he'd felt rather silly talking to an animal that most people would make into Christmas dinner. But the bird's owner, Kit's neighbor, had insisted that Moses had a personality and enjoyed conversation, and Moses had begun wandering over to Kit's farm on his own from time to time.

Apparently he liked the company here. And the stream that ran across one corner of the property. And the scratches. But he never seemed to be able to find his way back without a human escort.

Moses looked around, then met Kit's eyes and huffed a sigh.

"Home it is then, lad."

Kit started off toward Broadstone Farm, the home of Mr. and Mrs. Devereaux and their granddaughter, with Moses waddling along beside him.

Chapter 2

When Kit was halfway up the drive of Broadstone Farm, a woman dressed in a faded green gown and matching bonnet came around the side of the house and stopped, raising a hand to shade her eyes in their direction.

He waved at her. "That's your mama, I think," he said to the goose.

Moses continued to waddle stoically along beside Kit for another minute or two until the woman called to them.

"Moses? Is that you?"

The bird perked up at the sound and honked in return, his little webbed feet moving faster and faster until he was half running, half flying toward the woman.

"Indeed, that's your mama," Kit said with a chuckle, following along behind.

By the time he caught up to Moses, the woman was crouched down beside the goose scratching the back of his long neck. She gave him one last pat before rising.

"Ah, Mr. Mathison brought you home again," Miss Devereaux said to her pet, wiping her hand on her skirt. The bird must have been wet from the light rain that still fell. "Did you say thank you?"

"He never does," Kit replied with feigned exasperation. "I don't know what kind of bird you raised."

She laughed a little, even though they'd had this same exchange numerous times over the past two years. "I think he's jealous of your navigation skills. You can find your way back and forth between our two homes without any help at all. For all his intelligence, Moses still hasn't quite mastered that skill yet."

Kit smiled in return, wondering briefly if this would be the sum of their relationship from now on—small talk about a bird. "Well, his timing was good today. I needed to get away for a while."

"Oh?"

"My roof caved in."

Miss Devereaux gasped, her eyes widening. "No!"

"On top of me. While I was sleeping."

"Oh, Kit," she breathed.

He started momentarily at the use of his nickname. In the time since he'd moved back into his childhood home she'd only ever called him "Mr. Mathison," despite having called him "Kit" for all the years they spent in each other's company growing up.

"How awful. Come inside and sit down for a moment or two, won't you? Have you eaten yet this morning? Grandmère is just about to put breakfast on the table."

Mrs. Devereaux could make shoe leather taste good, and Kit put a hand to his empty stomach. "I believe I will. It's too hard to think when one is hungry."

He followed Miss Devereaux and Moses up to the house where the bird veered off toward the barn, and the two humans entered the kitchen where the smell of eggs frying in butter washed over them.

Kit's stomach growled.

"Grandmère, we have one more for breakfast," Miss Devereaux said to the gray-haired woman at the stove, removing her bonnet and hanging it on a peg behind the door. She pushed a lock of glossy brown hair behind her ear. "Mr. Mathison has had a trying start to his day, and I've asked him to join us."

Mrs. Devereaux slid the pan she was tending to a cooler part of the stove. "Christopher," she said with a bright smile, enunciating each syllable of his name in her French accent. "How good it is to see you!"

He swept his hat off his head and bowed like a proper English gentleman, but couldn't keep the grin from his face.

"Madame Devereaux, the pleasure is all mine. What can I do to help?"

Mrs. Devereaux directed him to a towel and the stack of plates behind her. He gathered them up after drying his hands and followed Miss Devereaux out to the dining room.

"How bad is the roof?" she asked, laying forks and knives next to the plates he set out.

Kit's shoulder slumped. "There's a hole a couple of feet across that goes through the roof, into the attic, and through the ceiling. And it looks like there are a few weak spots elsewhere."

"That sounds like fairly extensive damage." Two forks clinked together in her hand as she separated them. "Will you need a completely new roof?"

"I won't know for certain until I can get a builder out to have a look," he set the last plate down and looked over at her, "but it seems likely. Until then, I'll have to cover the holes as best I can and hope the rain lets up."

Miss Devereaux met his gaze. "Less rain would be ideal, yes. In the meantime, you can't stay in a house with a hole in the roof, especially when it's so wet."

"What was that?" Mr. Devereaux asked, entering the dining room as his granddaughter headed back to the kitchen. "Christopher has a hole in his roof?"

Kit recounted the events of the morning for Miss Devereaux's grandfather, trying to keep his voice matter of fact when his mind was spinning.

"Sylvie is right, you cannot stay in that house again until it's properly repaired." The smell of bacon permeated the room and he waited a moment for Mrs. Devereaux to enter the room with a platter of sizzling hot food. Then he continued, "You should stay here for a few nights."

Mrs. Devereaux's eyes met her husband's and she nodded. "Yes, I was thinking the same thing."

Miss Devereaux followed her grandmother in with four cups. "What?"

"What?" Kit said at the same time.

Mr. Devereaux took the platter of food and set it on the table, then held out a chair for his wife. "You'll have a warm, dry place to sleep until your bedchamber is serviceable again," he said to Kit, as if the decision had been made.

"That does make sense," Miss Devereaux added, taking her seat at the table. "And we have plenty of room."

Kit looked at the three of them, offering up their home to him as if it was something they did every day. It was true they'd known him since he was in leading strings, but the years he'd spent in Scotland after his father died had added a measure of reserve to their relationship that they had yet to fully put aside.

"Thank you," he said simply, pulling out his own chair and settling himself at the table. "I will spend the day assessing and cleaning and patching, and I'll join you for supper tonight."

Mrs. Devereaux smiled brightly. "Excellent."

Mr. Devereaux nodded once and turned his attention to his food.

Kit's eyes met Miss Devereaux's and he smiled to cover the flash of longing that washed over him. Would these couple of days be awkward between him and Sylvie? Or could they perhaps use this physical proximity to start rebuilding their friendship?

Sylvie sat across the table from Mr. Mathison once again that evening, wanting to inquire about the state of his house—and himself. But his speech was slow and his eyelids drooped, and he excused himself to bed not long after they'd sat down. She led him up the stairs and down the hallway to the extra bedchamber she'd helped her grandmother prepare earlier in the day. He mumbled his thanks and disappeared inside, closing the door behind him.

The second evening of his stay, Mr. Mathison managed some small talk at supper but was otherwise quiet, almost dull—wholly unlike the boy she remembered from her childhood.

Of course, the boy never had to worry about the time and expense involved in repairing his crumbling home.

He once again excused himself to bed early, and Sylvie watched him trudge up the stairs alone, wondering what she could do to make him feel better. She turned the thought over in her mind as she cleared the table and washed the dishes, unsure of what kind of gesture would be welcome. They had been friends as children due to the proximity of their homes, but not overly close ones. Kit was the eldest son of an English landowner, while Sylvie's grandparents were immigrants who paid for the privilege of running Broadstone.

The two families hadn't exactly moved in the same social circles.

But Kit had always been kind to her, and they had spent some time together as affable companions when they were children and into their adolescence. She grinned momentarily remembering the time Kit had wanted to learn to bake a cake and her grandmother had obliged him, showing him how to measure out ingredients, what to mix together when, and how hot the oven needed to be. With Grandmère's guidance, Kit's cake had been a tasty treat. When he'd repeated the action at home the following week, it had resulted in a blackened brick.

"Do we have any of that pound cake left?" she asked herself aloud, wiping her hands on her apron and searching through the larder. "Ah-ha!" She found half of the pound cake her grandmother had made the day before and a few undersized strawberries from the kitchen garden. "That will do just fine."

Sylvie waited for her grandparents to go up to bed, then waited another quarter of an hour. She crept quietly into the kitchen and cut two slices of pound cake, then carried them slowly up the stairs.

Was he even awake?

There was a faint light shining under his door, and she took a chance, knocking softly. "Mr. Mathison?"

There was a rustle of fabric and the creak of the floor, then the door swung open. "Miss Devereaux? Is everything all right?"

"Yes, everything is fine." She offered him one of the plates. "I only thought that if you were still up, you might like some cake."

He glanced from her to the plate, then back to her, and a wide smile spread across his face. "That was very thoughtful, thank you." When he accepted the plate and took a bite of the cake, his features melted into an expression that was part bliss and part relief. "This is so good."

"Grandmère's special recipe," Sylvie replied with a smile of her own. It was good to see him happy, even if it was only for a moment.

Mr. Mathison chuckled, leaning against the door frame. "Do you remember the time she tried to teach me to bake?"

"Yes," Sylvie grinned, taking a bite of her own piece of cake. "The first one turned out rather well, if I recall."

"But not the second." He breathed in and let out a long sigh. "I fear the same thing is happening with the house, and that I'm not as good at taking care of my home as I should be."

Sylvie almost made a joke in an attempt to return the joy to his face, but elected not to. Perhaps he needed a sympathetic ear more than a quick smile. "Is it that bad?"

"I think it might be." He took another bite of cake and chewed it slowly. "I will know for certain in three days when the builder comes out, but I already know that it will not be good."

She wanted to reach out and touch him, to try to impart whatever comfort to him that she could. But she didn't know how to do that for him anymore. In that moment, she wasn't sure she ever did know. Instead, she said, "You can stay here as long as you need to. I know it's not the same as sleeping in your own bed in your own home..."

"But I very much appreciate your kindness," he finished for her. "These past few days have been exhausting. Coming home to good food, a dry bed, and people who care about me has been exactly the thing I need to keep going."

Sylvie's gaze dropped to the floor for the briefest of moments before meeting his blue eyes again in the dim light emanating from his bedchamber. "I'm glad we could provide that for you."

They stood in a slightly awkward silence for another moment before she spoke again. "I should seek my bed. I may not have a leaky house to repair, but I do have a list of tasks as long as my arm to start in the morning."

He gave her a half-bow, holding tight to his cake plate. "Good night, Miss Devereaux."

"Good night, Mr. Mathison."

Kit said goodbye to the builder and headed slowly for Broadstone Farm. When he was about halfway up the drive, Moses came waddling toward him, honking a greeting.

"I'm glad one of us is in good spirits," he told the bird, stooping to scratch the base of Moses's neck.

The pair walked up to the house together in companionable silence and met Miss Devereaux, who was sitting in the grass with her back against the rough bark of a large oak tree. She raised her eyebrows in an unasked question, and Kit sat down beside her as the leaves rustled quietly in the slight breeze.

"The whole roof has to be replaced."

"Oh no."

"And the amount of time it will take will depend largely on the weather."

It was dry currently, but there were thick gray clouds gathering on the horizon, and Miss Devereaux's brown eyes shifted to them. "Oh no," she repeated with a note of dread.

It was the same feeling he'd had when the builder had broken the news. Putting a new roof on a house in the summer should have been a fairly straightforward procedure, but this summer had been everything except straightforward.

"Well," she continued, returning her gaze to him, "I meant what I said the other night. You can stay with us as long as you have the need."

He turned his body toward hers and offered her a small smile. "Thank you."

Chapter 3

"LET ME GET THAT ONE," Kit said, stooping to heft a large rock before Mr. Devereaux could make the attempt. They were repairing a stone wall that separated Broadstone Farm from the property behind it, but Mr. Devereaux was the embodiment of a willing spirit with weak flesh.

Instead of loudly lamenting the loss of his strength over the years, as some men might, Mr. Devereaux took a step back and leaned against a sound part of the wall. "You're welcome to it, Christopher."

Kit scooped the rock up and nestled it carefully into place, then picked up two smaller rocks to fill in holes on either side.

Mr. Devereaux watched him appraisingly. "I was young and strong like you once," he said with a note of wistfulness.

"I think you were stronger," Kit replied with a grin, bending his knees to heave another large rock into place. "Those didn't put themselves there."

Mr. Devereaux's eyes followed Kit's to a series of small boulders that served as the foundation of the wall. "Ah yes, I remember setting those. You and Sylvie must have been, what? Eight? Nine? And you wanted to climb on them after I put them in place."

The laugh escaped Kit before he could suppress it. "I remember that! Sylvie asked me to help her climb up, then challenged me to a race, with her on the boulders and me on the ground."

"Yes," the older man grinned, his eyes crinkling up at the corners. "She fell off the second one, but wouldn't give up!"

"She gets that from you, I think," Kit chuckled. "Never one to give up if there's a still a chance."

Mr. Devereaux sobered, leaning more heavily against the wall. "And a blessing it's been these past few years. We haven't had all the help we've needed since her parents went back to France, but my Sylvie does everything that she can to keep the farm and the house running."

"Well, perhaps I can relieve some of the burden while I'm here," Kit replied, continuing to fit rocks together and build up the wall.

Mr. Devereaux nodded thoughtfully. "We would very much appreciate that, including Sylvie. She should be getting her animals ready for the Harvest Festival. She takes at least one prize every year, but she's been too busy this year." His eyes met Kit's and held them. "When she's not working in the house or on the farm, she has begun to take in mending and sewing for some of the bachelors in the area. She has a friend in the village that she visits when she drops things off to her customers there, but it makes me sad that even her social engagements involve her working somehow."

Kit paused, resting his hand on the wall. "How long have things been this bad?"

"We have had to tighten the purse string the past few years, but this year..." Mr. Devereaux's whole face sagged.

He didn't have to finish the sentence. The ever-present rain was the first thing anyone spoke about after "How do you do?"

Kit nodded and resumed piling rocks in strategic places on the wall. He was a member of this household now, even if only temporarily, and his mind searched for ways he could provide some comfort to the people who offered him sanctuary. They wouldn't take money, even though he was effectively a boarder and should be paying for the privilege, but perhaps he could purchase some things they needed in addition to offering his labor.

And maybe he could find a way to remind Miss Devereaux what it was like to be carefree. For some reason, that felt very important to him.

Kit packed that feeling away for examination another time and said instead, "As long as I'm here, I'll do whatever I can to be helpful."

"You always were a good boy, Christopher," Mr. Devereaux said, his features lightening considerably. "And it appears you've grown up to be a good man."

"My mother will be pleased you think so."

"How is your mother?"

They talked of family and old times for a while longer while Kit continued to repair the stone wall, fitting rocks into crevices just the right size. When a light drizzle began to fall and the rocks became slippery, Mr. Devereaux declared that work was done for the day and that they should head back to the house.

Miss Devereaux's voice greeted them when they entered the kitchen. "I picked up the post while I was in the village, Grandpère. There's a letter from Papa." She shifted the wooden spoon she was stirring something with to her other hand and met Kit's gaze. "There's a letter for you, too, Mr. Mathison."

"Oh?"

Kit followed Mr. Devereaux to the stack of letters on the dining room table and grinned the moment he laid eyes on his. The handwriting was that of his best friend turned sister-in-law, Maddie, who had written to him regularly after his family had left Kent for Scotland and continued to do so now that they lived considerably closer together. He took it up to his bedchamber, washing his face and hands and putting on a clean shirt before returning to the dining room to help set the table for supper.

After the food was eaten and the table cleared, Mr. and Mrs. Devereaux settled themselves before the fire, and Miss Devereaux sat down on the sofa to sew some buttons onto a shirt. Kit retrieved his letter and brought it down, seating himself at the other end of the sofa near the oil lamp and cracking open the plain seal.

He must have had a serious expression, because Mrs. Devereaux turned to him after a few moments and asked, "Is everything well, Christopher?"

"Hmm? Oh, yes." He grinned. "My brother's wife has written to tell me about the repairs he's made to their home. He managed to re-hang a door, and there was much celebrating."

"Thomas married Maddie Hayward, didn't he?" Miss Devereaux asked, glancing up from her sewing.

Kit nodded. "He did. They live with her grandmother about two hours' ride from here."

"Who is she?" Mrs. Devereaux inquired. "That name sounds familiar."

"Her parents are Kit's neighbors on the other side. You should remember Maddie, Grandmère," Miss Devereaux prompted. "She was Kit's closest friend when we were children. The one who—" She stopped abruptly and pressed her lips together.

Kit put his letter down and turned his gaze on her, filing away the feeling that washed over him when she called him "Kit," and chuckling when she looked away with an awkward smile. "The one who everyone thought *I* was going to marry," he said slyly. "Is that what you were going to say?"

Miss Devereaux nodded sheepishly and Mrs. Devereaux's eyes lit with recognition. "I remember her now. She was the one who caught a fish bigger than Christopher's, yes?"

Miss Devereaux laughed aloud, then hastily covered her mouth with one hand to stifle it. "I'd forgotten about the fish," she said after a moment, dropping her hand into her lap. "You sulked here for days when that happened."

"But you took me in and comforted me," Kit replied, the memory of Sylvie's arm around him, the biscuits Mrs. Devereaux had given them, forming in his mind. "Then promptly told me to go congratulate Maddie on her catch."

Miss Devereaux grinned. "To your credit, you did exactly that."

Mrs. Devereaux turned back to her husband to ask him a question, and Miss Devereaux leaned toward Kit. "Grandpère told me about how you helped him with the stone wall today, or rather, how you did all the labor. Is there something I can do to return the favor?"

Kit's first instinct was to say no, that he was the one who owed them and hadn't done it in order to get something in return. But perhaps he could give her the chance to slow down and relax while still feeling useful. "I could use some help with some new arrivals in my barn, and you've always been good with animals. Can you go over with me tomorrow?"

She thought for a moment, then nodded slowly. "As long as I'm back in time to help prepare supper."

"Excellent."

They talked about unimportant things for a while longer while she sewed, then Kit excused himself to his chamber. Climbing the stairs two at a time, he held in his mind that picture of a young Sylvie, who had been there for him when he'd needed a friend, and told him when he needed to discard his childishness. It had been exactly what he needed.

Could he be what she needed now?

Sylvie entered Mr. Mathison's barn beside him, with Moses close on their heels. "What can I do?" she asked, casting her eyes over the large interior.

"Will you take a look at these kittens?" he asked, gesturing to a nest of hay in one of the horse boxes. "This is the mother's first litter, and I don't think she quite knows how to care for them."

"Of course. Let's see what we have here..." She entered the horse box and knelt down just close enough to see the kittens, but not close enough to upset their mother, her heart swelling at the sight of their tiny faces. "Do you know how old they are?"

"A fortnight, I think," came the reply as he approached and knelt down beside her. The heat radiating from his body felt good in the cool damp air.

Sylvie nodded, watching the mother cat approach her and sniff at the hem of her skirt. Moses, she noted, had gone off to another part of the barn. "Their eyes are all open but they're still very small, so that fits."

The mother, a stocky tortoiseshell cat, approached Mr. Mathison, sniffed him briefly, then rubbed her body against his legs. "Good morning, Leto," he responded, scratching her back gently. "This is Sylvie. She's a friend. Would you mind if she looked over your babies?"

Sylvie instinctively suppressed the smile that threatened to form on her lips, then realized what she was doing and relaxed her expression. "How do you do, Leto?"

The cat rubbed on Mr. Mathison one more time, then eyed Sylvie as if to judge whether or not her kittens were safe with this stranger.

"You have so many babies!" Sylvie continued, slowly stretching out a hand toward Leto. "Do you need help looking after them?"

Leto sniffed Sylvie's fingers, then took a few steps toward her and pushed herself against Sylvie's palm. Sylvie reciprocated by scratching Leto's neck and was rewarded when the cat arched up into her hand.

"I think she likes you," Mr. Mathison said cheerfully.

"You trust me, so she's decided to trust me...for the moment," Sylvie replied, scratching Leto's face. "I'm going to take a look at your babies now, Leto, but I promise I won't hurt them."

Sylvie slowly made her way toward the nest in the hay, keeping one eye on Leto lest she decide to strike out in defense of her young. Leto, too, kept her eyes on Sylvie, moving with her as she peered over the edge of the nest. There were seven in total: one tortoiseshell like her mother, two orange toms, three gray-and-whites, and a diminutive all-black that appeared to be the runt of the litter.

Her knees began to protest and Sylvie carefully shifted to a new position sitting in the hay, locking eyes with Mr. Mathison for a moment before reaching into the nest and picking up the black kitten.

Leto watched Sylvie intently with wide green eyes.

"Don't worry," Mr. Mathison said gently, stroking the cat.

One by one, Sylvie lifted and studied each kitten, checking their overall condition, to see if they were getting enough to eat and being cleaned properly. Each time Leto got too tense, Mr. Mathison would touch her, or scratch her in her favorite spot, and she'd relax again.

"Here you are, Leto," Sylvie said, placing the last kitten back in the nest, "I'm quite finished now."

She rose with Mr. Mathison's help and brushed the hay from her skirt as Leto went immediately to her kittens and began to bathe them.

"How do they look?" Mr. Mathison asked, leading her out of the horse box.

"Fairly good," she responded, noting that he didn't release her hand until they were halfway to the entrance of the barn. Last time he'd held her hand they'd been perhaps ten years old. "The black one is a bit on the small side, even for as young as they are, and Leto isn't cleaning them overly well. But on the whole they look normal for their age."

A sigh of relief whooshed out of Mr. Mathison and he put a hand to his chest. "Oh good. They looked awfully small to me, and I was afraid she wasn't feeding them properly."

Most people wouldn't think twice about a litter of barn cats, and Sylvie found his concern touching. "I can show you how to clean them up, and how to feed the black one to make sure she's getting enough to eat, if you'd like."

"Excellent," he grinned. "Will you help me look after them? When you have a spare moment, of course."

Sylvie's mind traveled over the list of tasks she needed to complete each day and sighed inwardly. She didn't really have time to take on another responsibility. But it wouldn't really be her responsibility—Mr. Mathison would be doing the lion's share of the work. "Help Kit with his kittens?" she asked spontaneously, then giggled. "I could do that."

"I'll make it worth your while," he answered with a grin, offering her his arm and leading her toward the house. "Wait until you see…"

She clasped his arm firmly and allowed him to whisk her into his kitchen, where he had laid out a cold luncheon on the table.

"What is this?"

"A meal that you didn't have to prepare."

She took in the slices of bread and block of cheese, the plate of what looked like ham flanked by four oranges.

Wait. Oranges?

"Where did these come from?" she asked, letting go of his arm to pick up an orange and inspect it as closely as she had the kittens.

"From a friend of mine who keeps an orange tree in his conservatory," Mr. Mathison answered, closing the gap between them again. "I thought you might enjoy them."

She tilted her head back to meet his blue eyes. They hadn't had much interaction in the two years he'd been back, outside of him walking Moses back home. Was he still the boy she'd capered with when they were children? The one who had made a point of continuing their friendship into adolescence despite the difference in their stations?

"If not, I'll be happy to eat them all myself.," he continued, his baritone voice breaking her train of thought.

She laughed lightly—that sounded like the old Kit. "That was very thoughtful of you. Thank you."

He handed her a plate and picked one up for himself, pausing when a series of loud bangs filled the room. "How do you feel about eating outdoors? Then we won't have to listen to the noise of the builder's men working on the house."

She agreed and, after serving herself, followed him outside and across the farm. "Where are we going?"

"You'll see."

She briefly considered taking his arm again—she craved the feeling of safety and comfort that came with his touch—but couldn't ascertain how to do so while holding an orange and a plate. Instead, she inched closer to him as they walked, taking care not to get so close they would bump into each other, but close enough to detect the scent of hay that clung to his clothing.

"Here we are," he proclaimed, stopping at the edge of a stream. "And look! Someone has left a bottle of lemonade here in the cold water."

Kit set his food down and pulled a stone bottle out of the cool water, shaking the drops from his hand and holding it out to her.

"You planned this."

"I did," he grinned. His expression sobered a bit, and he continued, "I know you have a long list of things that need to be done, but you never seem to have any time to just rest."

She didn't reply for several moment, trying to discern what exactly she was feeling. Her grandparents, her friends, they were all wonderful, generous people. But when was the last time anyone had thought to provide her with the luxury of *rest*?

Sylvie set her plate and orange on the ground and took the cold bottle, uncorking the top and breathing in the sweet, lemony smell with a soft smile.

"Thank you," she said again, her voice full of emotions she still couldn't name. "This is a tremendous gift."

His eyes caught hers and held them. "It's my pleasure to give it."

They sat on the grassy bank of the stream under a cloudy sky, eating in companionable silence as the water bubbled along beside them and the birds called back and forth to each other. Sylvie forced the list of tasks from her mind, the tension in her shoulders slowly releasing with every sip of lemonade.

It was exactly what she had needed.

Chapter 4

For the next several weeks, Sylvie continued her regular routine with the addition of visits to Kit's barn to check on the kittens. It was difficult to justify spending the time away when there was so much to be done, but Sylvie found herself looking forward to the visits, particularly since Kit went to the trouble of providing a quiet luncheon by the stream when the weather allowed, and in his own kitchen when the rain returned.

The kittens grew strong and healthy, including the little black runt, and they were great fun to play with, of course. But sitting with Kit, sometimes talking about their shared past, sometimes speculating about the future, was a somewhat unexpected delight.

Especially when he answered her impertinent questions.

"Why did you never marry Maddie Hayward?" she asked one day. "I always thought you would."

Kit was lying on his back, his plate empty beside him, gazing up at a rare blue sky. "She was my closest friend—she still is—but what we share isn't romantic. I did offer once, though."

"You did? When?"

When Kit didn't elaborate, Sylvie poked him in the shoulder. "You can't just say you once offered for Maddie and leave it at that. What happened? Or," she continued somewhat hastily, "is it too painful to speak of?"

Kit shook his head. "No pain at all, in fact. It was over two years ago now, and she despaired of ever finding a husband because everyone thought she was waiting for me to speak. I told her that if she wanted to marry me, I would be willing. That's all."

"But she wed your brother instead."

"Yes," he confirmed with a grin. "They hatched some plan together to free her from everyone's expectations, and ended up falling in love."

Sylvie sighed, her mouth curving into a dreamy smile. "How lovely. And you're truly not bothered?"

Kit rolled onto his side and met her gaze with another smile, this one softer. "Not at all. They are two of my favorite people in the world, and I'm glad they've found happiness together."

Sylvie opened her mouth to reply but caught Moses waddling toward them out of the corner of her eye. "I suppose we should get back to the house," she said instead, reaching for their plates and the stone bottle with the last of the lemonade.

Kit flopped onto his back once more and sighed heavily. "Yes, I suppose we should."

He helped her gather up their things and carry them to his kitchen, then walked beside her back to Broadstone Farm with Moses between them. Sylvie found herself wanting to reach out to Kit, to hold his hand or take his arm, but judged both actions too intimate for now.

Maybe in the future...

The Devereaux home was strangely silent when they entered with no sign of Grandmère, who was usually working in the kitchen at this time of the day. Sylvie exchanged a look with Kit and instinctively took a step closer to him.

"What's wrong?" he asked quietly.

"I'm not sure. But something isn't right."

She crept through the house, Kit close behind her, and finally stumbled upon Grandmère standing in the sitting room with her face in her hands, Grandpère with his arms about her. Sylvie immediately turned to leave, but Grandpère motioned them to come into the room.

"This effects you both, too."

"What's happened?" Sylvie asked, grateful for the support Kit's presence lent.

Grandpère took in a breath and let it out slowly, releasing his wife. "There will be no crop this year."

The room began to spin, and Sylvie couldn't make it stop. "Nothing?"

Grandpère shook his head. "Not a single stalk of wheat. It's all rotted."

Sylvie rocked backward slightly, but was steadied by the warm pressure of a hand on her back. Her mind was spinning as fast as the room, and she closed her eyes to concentrate better. "I have some money from—"

Grandpère raised a hand to stop her. "We will make plans later. Right now, let us simply come to terms with it."

But for Sylvie, making plans and trying to solve the problem were what helped her come to terms with bad news. And, though not unexpected, this was still the worst news she'd ever been given.

"I'm going to take a walk," she said as Grandpère went back to consoling Grandmère.

"Would you like some company? Or would you rather be alone?"

Kit's voice was gruff but strong, and pierced her heart. "Company would be nice," she managed thickly. The last thing she wanted right now was to be alone.

They walked out through the kitchen and Sylvie automatically started toward the wheat field, but halted. She couldn't bear to look at the rotted plants wasting away in the soggy ground.

Kit came to the rescue. "Why don't we walk over to the stream?"

She nodded, numbness replacing the spinning feeling she'd experienced inside the house.

They walked without speaking, arms brushing from time to time with the rhythm of their steps, the singing songbirds and sun shining brightly overhead irritating Sylvie like a grain of sand in her eye. Why did the sun have to show itself today of all days? Didn't it realize her world was about to end?

The first fat tear rolled down her face, and was followed by another and another in short succession. She brushed them away but they were replaced by a sudden horde of others, flowing down her cheeks and splashing onto the bodice of her dress.

Kit took her hand and pulled her to a gentle stop, then pulled her to him and enveloped her in his arms. Sylvie sunk into his embrace, circling her own arms around him and holding him tightly against her as she sobbed.

"What are we going to do?"

Late that night, after Mr. and Mrs. Devereaux had gone to bed, Kit sat beside Sylvie on the worn brown couch in the sitting room with only their clasped hands between them. The fire burned low, throwing off little light, but neither had bothered to light a candle or lamp to lessen the darkness.

Kit breathed slowly in, then let out the breath with as little sound as possible. He was grateful for the dark, truth be told—it gave him a measure of courage for what he was about to do.

"Sylvie," he said softly, hoping she couldn't hear the slight shaking in his voice. "I know you're worried about what will become of your home..."

She turned to face him, the outline of her nose and mouth visible in the dim light but her eyes were lost in shadow. "But you have an idea," she finished for him.

Was she smiling? Was she tense? He couldn't tell, but he plunged ahead. "Yes. I was thinking that if you and I were wed, all our problems would be solved."

She didn't reply immediately, but her fingers tensed around his. "How would our problems be solved?"

"Well, for one thing, I can pay the rent for Broadstone," he said, trying to infuse more confidence into his voice. "You and I could live here if your grandparents were amenable, and I could have some other repairs done on my house while the work continues on the roof."

She was nodding slowly, but didn't speak.

"Once the repairs on my house were completed, you and I could live there. You'd still be close to your grandparents and able to help out if they needed you, or us. But they would have their privacy and we would have ours."

She stilled, and replied quietly. "If you marry me, you are tied to me until one of us dies."

"Yes, I know that." He grinned, though she likely couldn't see it. "I am tied to you by friendship already. One more bond will not change things all that much."

Sylvie's hand slipped from his. "You don't think *marriage* would change our relationship?"

Kit started to speak but stopped, turning his hand palm up on the sofa. "Practically speaking, things would not be so different, no. Emotionally, though..." He paused. What exactly did he think would happen if Sylvie became his wife? "I would hope that marriage would add another dimension to our relationship."

She nodded again once, and Kit desperately wished he could see the expression on her face. Was she happy? Shocked? Insulted?

"You have property that you'll want to pass down," she finally said, her voice carefully even. "Do you anticipate having children?"

This question Kit was prepared for. "My property is not entailed, so I can leave it to whomever I wish."

"But do you *want* to have children?" Sylvie repeated slowly.

Well, perhaps he wasn't as prepared as he thought. "I always expected to, but no one has ever asked me what I wanted. Do you want to have children?"

"Yes," she answered without hesitation. "If my health and our family finances could support such a notion, I think I'd like to have a large family."

"Oh." The word fell from his mouth before he could think of a better response, but he really didn't know what else to say. Sylvie would make a wonderful mother, certainly, and being a father would be an adventure to look forward to. But he'd have to bed Sylvie to get her with child.

They hadn't even kissed yet.

What would it be like with Sylvie? Would it be a chore, like it was for some of his friends and their wives? Would it be awkward because they had known each other as children? Or could it be pleasurable, even fun?

"You haven't really thought this through, have you?" she asked, disrupting his thoughts. "Is this what happened when you asked Maddie, too? Do you just go around asking women to marry you to help them out of a difficult situation?"

Kit bristled a bit at that. "Perhaps I didn't give it the consideration it was due, but I did not make this offer lightly. I think you and I could make a good life together, and our marriage *would* solve several problems for both of us."

"But those things you listed—you paying rent on the farm, living here while your house is repaired, moving back into your house when it's ready but still being available to help out here—those can all happen even if we never see the inside of a church together."

"Oh." Apparently that was going to be his standard response to everything she told him now.

She turned toward him, lacing her fingers together as she slung one elbow over the back of the sofa. "Did that truly never occur to you? Or did you simply want me to be your wife and the circumstances made it convenient to ask?"

She sounded curious now, and Kit was rather curious himself. "Honestly?"

"Please."

"I believe it was some of both." He longed to take her hand again, to stroke her hair, to have her in his arms, but instead he settled his hands on his knees. "I miss the friendship that we used to have, and if we were wed we'd have the opportunity to spend more time together. I also want very much to help you and your family keep your home."

Sylvie placed her hand on his for a brief moment, then rose from the sofa. "I appreciate your candor, and your generosity toward my family, Kit, but I can't marry you. Not this way."

She lingered a moment longer then headed toward the staircase, leaving Kit alone in the dark with his thoughts.

Sylvie closed the door to her bedchamber with a sigh that was half fatigue and half bewilderment. The fire that she'd laid earlier in the evening burned cheerily in the fireplace, casting long, flickering shadows over everything in the room.

Kit had asked her to marry him.

Kit had asked her to marry him!

He said he meant it, and that it wasn't only a convenient way to solve their financial problems. But Kit's circle of acquaintances included several rungs of society that Sylvie, the granddaughter of glorified tenant farmers, could never aspire to. Perhaps he expected to have a more formal alliance with his wife, where they would come together for procreation and light conversation, and live their separate lives the rest of the time.

But Sylvie wanted her husband to be her partner, her lover, not just a man she was legally bound to.

She leaned back against the door and sighed again, this time with the tiniest bit of disappointment. It was unlikely Kit could be that man to her, though a part of her wanted to explore the idea. What would it be like to have their half-opened flower of a friendship blossom into a strong, devoted partnership? To know that he loved her and held her best interests in his heart, and that she reciprocated those feelings?

To know what it was like to be kissed by Kit, touched and caressed, to lie with him in the bed they shared...

She shook herself mentally and pushed away from the door. She was not going to marry Kit, to gamble her future on a fantasy coming true, so none of those things mattered.

What mattered was figuring out how to pay the rent this quarter for the farm.

Chapter 5

HEAVY RAINS RAGED ACROSS KENT the next day, flooding the already sodden landscape and forcing Kit, Sylvie, and her grandparents to remain indoors. Sylvie spent most of her time on the sofa in the sitting room mending clothes, and Kit tried desperately to occupy himself in ways that didn't include watching her. He finally resorted to going through his accounts, spreading out the big leather-bound books and various other papers on the table in the dining room with a deep sigh that was equal parts regret and resignation.

Kit's inheritance from his father was, strictly speaking, an estate. The parcel of land he owned was large enough to require account books and a man of business, but not large enough for him to rank among the more important landed gentry. He had the house and farm, and just a few small investments—plenty to live on when times were good, but lately he'd begun to economize in order to afford the repairs required on the house.

As he worked his way through the columns and papers, though, he knew he'd need to do more than economize this time.

He must have groaned aloud, for the door opened and Sylvie came in, her eyebrows raised and her mouth drawn into a frown. "Is everything alright?"

He blew out a breath, pushing away the awkwardness of seeing the woman who'd rejected his proposal of marriage just the day before. She was still his friend, and he needed a friend right now. "No."

"Would you like to talk about it?"

A small smile tugged at his mouth. This must have been difficult for her, too, perhaps even embarrassing. But when she thought he needed help, she was there to offer it.

Kit pulled out a chair near his and gestured for her to sit down. "My crops have failed, too," he began. "There might be enough to harvest for personal use, but there certainly isn't enough there to sell, so I'll have no income from the fields this year."

" 'From the fields' meaning you'll have income from other sources?"

"Yes, exactly." He picked up a letter he'd received the previous day from his man of business. He'd tossed it on the wash stand in his chamber and blithely went about asking for Sylvie's hand, forgetting all about it until he sat down with his account books. "The estate could survive a bad yield or a year with no yield at all—I made sure of that. But this..."

She took the letter when he offered it to her and read silently. After a moment, her eyes widened. "Oh, Kit. The whole ship?"

His father had regularly invested in the import of goods from outside the realm, a practice Kit was content to continue when he took the reins.

"I knew the risks," he said, a note of defeat creeping into his voice despite his efforts to keep it out. "Storms, pirates, blockades—there are many ways a ship's cargo can be lost. I thought it was a risk worth taking, but now..."

"Now you've lost your whole crop and this investment," she finished, setting the letter on the table. For a moment he thought she would touch him, possibly to comfort him, but her hand slid into her own lap instead.

"And I'll have to lower the tenants' rents so they can afford to remain in their homes. Perhaps it's good that you refused me, Sylvie," he said quietly. "I can't do any of the things I promised you now."

She shook her head, tutting at him like an old hen. "If you think my only interest in you was ever for your money, then it *is* a good thing I refused you. You ought to know me better than that."

He did know her better than that, and it was a stupid thing for him to say. But his fortune, while not large, had always been a point in his favor. Losing even part of it felt like a strike against him in everyone's eyes —including hers—regardless of their actual feelings towards him.

"I do. And I apologize," he managed, clearing his throat. "I'm not good company just now, I think. I'll..." Where could he go? He longed to go sit by the stream running across his meadow, but the weather was fit for neither man nor beast, so he was confined to the house. "I'll go lie down for a while."

She remained motionless in her chair as he gathered up his papers and account books, laying a hand on his back briefly as he exited the room. Once he made it to his bedchamber, he set his pile of work on the wash stand and flopped onto his bed, trying to still his swirling thoughts.

He could no longer provide financial security to Sylvie and her grandparents, nor any of the people who worked on the farm. He wasn't even sure he would be able to pay the builder for the work done on his roof. Could he keep the farm running without going into debt? Would anyone lend him money if he couldn't?

Kit rolled over and buried his face in the peacock blue quilt covering his bed so no one would hear him moan. Perhaps he would take a page from Mr. Devereaux's book and just come to terms with this loss before trying to find a solution.

If only he'd invested more carefully!

He laid there for a while, eventually turning onto his back again, staring up at the ceiling with unseeing eyes, ignoring the pelting of the rain against the windows. The only thing that seemed to quiet his mind was recalling the feel of Sylvie's hand on his back in the dining room, fleeting as the contact had been. It meant that she still cared about him, that she would be there if he needed her.

And he needed her now.

He clambered off the bed and flung open the door to his bedchamber, only to find Sylvie standing at the threshold.

"Sylvie?"

"Kit?"

He froze, his brain overwhelmed with the sheer number of actions he could take.

"Are you well?" she asked, slightly confused, and that seemed to break the spell.

He reached for her, sliding an arm around her waist and pulling her into the room. "Will you hold me for a while, Sylvie Devereaux? I need to borrow some of your strength."

Her arms came around his neck in a warm embrace, her cheek resting against his. "You may have all the strength I can give you."

The light pressure of Kit's hands on Sylvie's body, the soft sound of his breathing—his embrace was warm and comforting, even though she was supposed to be comforting him. The faint fragrance of Grandmère's homemade soap combined with the scent of his skin and slowly enveloped her, setting her heart off at a gallop. When he sighed deeply, his body relaxing around her as his chest rose and fell, she finally understood what other women meant when they talked about butterflies in their stomach.

She tightened her arms around his neck and combed her fingers through his short blond hair. "Stronger now?" she asked, her voice a near whisper as she tried to conceal the emotions coursing through her.

"I don't know how I'd face this on my own," he replied quietly.

"You don't have to. You never have to."

His heart was beating as fast as hers now—she could feel it reverberating through his body pressed against hers. Was he experiencing the same things she was? She pressed her lips to his temple, his cheek, and his breathing hitched.

"Sylvie..."

Her name was almost a moan, and it ignited a flame somewhere inside her. "Yes?"

His lips brushed her earlobe. "I want to kiss you," he whispered, his voice husky. "May I?"

"Yes," she breathed, closing her eyes as he repeated the sequence she started, kissing her temple, her cheek, then capturing her lips.

"Mmmmm." Her hands slid down his back and cupped his derriere.

He broke the kiss, his eyes wide. "I did not expect that."

"Do you not like that?"

"I do, actually," he said with a grin. "I just didn't think you'd do it. Is there something you like that I can do for you?"

Her mind whirled, but she stopped it with the thought of her grandparents sleeping just down the hall. "Yes, but you'd better not. Kiss me again and I'll say goodnight, then we can talk things over in the morning."

He did as she bid him, kissing her thoroughly before loosening his arms around her. "Goodnight, then, my Sylvie. I look forward to tomorrow."

He kissed her hand and opened the door for her, checking the hallway quickly before she crept quietly back to her own chamber.

"What was that?" she demanded of her small desk as loudly as she dared. "I went to see if he was well, and ended up kissing him!"

Her body was still hot from the embrace and she picked up a letter to fan herself. "This is merely a physical attraction, though. I don't love Kit, and he certainly doesn't love me." She paused and touched a finger to her lips, then dropped her hand. "No, it doesn't matter what it was or what it meant. We have to figure out how to save our homes."

She washed and undressed, donning her nightdress and climbing into bed. But sleep was elusive. Too much had happened in too short a time, and Sylvie was completely overwhelmed. She turned onto her stomach and buried her face in her pillow, pushing aside everything to focus on paying rent for the quarter. She had a bit of money saved from the extra mending she'd taken in, so that was a start. She knew that Grandpère and Grandmère had a little, too. They could talk tomorrow about how much the combined sum was and how much they would still need to raise.

Sylvie turned onto her side and suppressed tears. Her animals would have to be sold, there was no question now. But would they bring in enough?

She fretted through most of the night, only sleeping for a couple of hours before it was time to rise and begin another day. Fortunately, the first person she saw when she descended the staircase was her grandfather. Good. They could talk over their situation and Sylvie could stop thinking about Kit.

"Good morning, Grandpère," she said with as much cheer as she could muster.

"Good morning, ma chérie," he returned with equal enthusiasm. "Your grandmother and I would like to talk to you this morning."

A bolt of panic shot through Sylvie. Did they know about her tête-à-tête with Kit?

"Since Christopher has already gone out for the day," he continued, "we thought breakfast would be a good time to discuss our financial situation."

"Oh, yes of course." She tried not to visibly deflate, but her relief was surely noticeable. But there was nothing to be done about it now. "I have some ideas."

Grandpère smiled, a genuine expression of happiness despite their current trials. "I knew you would."

Sylvie followed him to the dining room where her grandmother was already waiting, and settled herself at the table. As they ate their eggs with the last small, watery vegetables from the kitchen garden, Sylvie and her grandparents talked about how much money they needed, how much they currently possessed, how much the animals were likely to fetch, and what would be the best way to sell them.

Sylvie noted the various amounts on a scrap of paper, adding in estimated earnings for Mr. Ross's mending and the pies Grandmère planned to bake for the tea shop in the village with what remained of last year's apples.

It still wasn't enough, but they were getting closer to their goal. Sylvie set her pencil on the table and blew out a breath. Perhaps they would be able to manage after all. She stood, gathering plates and silverware to take to the kitchen for washing, and felt some of the tension leave her shoulders.

"Wait," Grandpère said after the door closed behind Sylvie, "we must put something aside for the Harvest Festival."

Sylvie almost turned around to go back into the dining room, but Grandmère's voice had a hard edge to it when she replied that stopped Sylvie in her tracks, with the door to the dining room open a tiny crack.

"We don't—"

"I know," Grandpère interrupted. "But a few pennies for Sylvie to have fun, when she's given up all of her own money for us..."

They were silent for a long moment and Sylvie couldn't see them from her vantage point. They were likely giving each other the same meaningful looks they often traded during their evening conversations in front of the fireplace, trying to converse without giving away their thoughts to anyone else in the room.

Grandmère broke the silence. "You are right, of course. This winter will bring many hardships, and Sylvie should have what enjoyment she can find before then."

Sylvie quietly closed the door the rest of the way and leaned against it. Even now, when she was well into adulthood and they were facing terrible difficulties, her dear grandparents were plotting to ensure she had some fun.

She must make sure they found some enjoyment at the Harvest Festival, too.

Chapter 6

A WEEK LATER, THEY CAME for the animals. Grandpère and Kit had made joint arrangements to have their livestock transported to the temporary market set up for the Harvest Festival near the village. There was a rumor among the local farmers that the Duke of Alston was looking to add to his herds and flocks, and some of his wealthy friends might be, too. If it was true, Grandpère and Kit both had a chance of making the money they required.

As Sylvie had been the one to care for the Devereaux animals, she was tasked with supervising their removal and making sure a select few—a few chickens for eggs, a goat for milk, and Moses for himself—remained on the farm. She segregated the keepers into one corner of the barn and made sure all persons involved in the transaction knew which animals were to go and which were to remain on the farm.

The whole process took longer than she expected, but it seemed to go smoothly enough. The animals were loaded onto wagons with the appropriate tags, then the transporters headed down the road to repeat the whole procedure a second time. Sylvie resettled the chickens, goat, and Moses in their regular homes, then headed back to the house to help Grandmère with the extra baking.

"How are you holding up?" Grandmère asked when Sylvie entered the kitchen.

"It was sad to see them go," Sylvie replied, trying to keep her voice steady as she tied on her apron. "I always knew they'd be sold or butchered at some point, but..."

"But you took care of them every day of their lives," Grandmère said, putting a hand on Sylvie's shoulder. "It's not surprising you'd grow fond of them."

Sylvie covered her grandmother's hand with her own and gave it a squeeze. "I suppose not."

She kept herself busy for the rest of the day in an attempt to keep her mind from simultaneously missing her livestock and worrying about how much money they would bring in. After the pies were baked, she set about cleaning every inch of the house, then sat down to work on the dress she planned to wear to the Harvest Festival. It was in need of new cuffs, and she wanted to add some embroidery to the hem to hide the worn spots and give the garment a bit more adornment overall.

It wasn't until Grandmère interrupted her later that she realized she'd been working on her dress for hours.

"Has Christopher returned?" her grandmother asked.

Sylvie shook her head. "Not that I'm aware of, no."

"He's always come back to us in time for supper or sent word that he would be late," Grandmère replied, squeezing her hands together. "I wonder what has happened."

Sylvie put her needle down and flexed her fingers, wondering too. It wasn't like him to simply disappear. "Perhaps loading the livestock took longer than anticipated— ours certainly did. I'll walk over and see."

"Thank you, my dear."

Sylvie put away her sewing things and went first to the barn. The noise and heightened activity of the repairs at Kit's home had caused Moses a fair amount of distress, and the bird had elected to remain closer to home for the past week or so. But perhaps if he had an escort he'd feel more comfortable amid the hustle and bustle.

"Moses, would you like to go for a walk?" she called, entering the barn.

He normally would come running at the word "walk," but there was no sign of him. The chickens and goat were where she had left them earlier in the day, but Moses was not.

"Not so unusual," Sylvie said to the goat. "He's never been shy about going off on his own."

She searched the rest of the barn and the surrounding area, discovering several frogs socializing around a newly formed pond filled with rainwater and a hedgehog family passing by, but no Moses.

"Maybe he went to Kit's after all."

The doubt was evident in her voice, even to her own ears, but she couldn't think of a better explanation. Well, then she would go to Kit's to look for her friend *and* her pet.

She covered the distance between the two homes in record time, stopping partway up the drive to catch her breath.

"Sylvie?"

Kit's large frame came down the drive and stopped before her. "Is everything alright?"

"I've solved one mystery," she said with a half-smile. "It's nearly time for supper, and Grandmère was worried that you hadn't returned."

Kit grinned, offering his arm to her. "Your grandmother was worried? But not you?"

She hesitated for half of a second, then took his arm and walked with him up the drive. It was the first time since their late night kiss that they had touched each other, were alone together. They'd continued to live in the same house, of course, but between the added work of selling the livestock and the presence of her grandparents, there had been no time for a private discussion.

She glanced up the drive at the horde of people either loading up the last of Kit's animals or working on the house. They weren't alone now either.

"I was curious," Sylvie answered, trying to push the feeling of Kit's lips on her skin out of her mind, "and now I've found you."

"Excellent. What's the other mystery? You said I was one."

She held his arm just a bit tighter. "Moses is missing. He hasn't come here, has he?"

"I don't think so. At least, I haven't seen him. But let's have a look." The last wagon of livestock trundled down the drive, and Kit steered Sylvie to one side, using the movement to disguise his light kiss on her temple. "We'll find him."

They searched the grounds, questioning each member of the builder's crew and Kit's laborers they came across.

"He should be pretty memorable," Sylvie pointed out after a half dozen men didn't remember seeing the bird, "you don't keep geese, so it's not as if there were a flock he could have disappeared into."

"You don't keep geese, Mr. Mathison?" one of the nearby farm hands asked. "Not even one?"

"Have you seen one?" Kit countered quickly. "Miss Devereaux is correct—the

Mathisons have never kept geese, but we are currently looking for one who was all on his own."

The farm hand's eyes widened. "One all by himself? I put him on one of the early wagons."

Sylvie gasped, but Kit remained calm. "Do you remember which wagon? What else was on it?"

The farm hand gave Kit as much information as he could recall before Kit sent him to saddle a horse. He turned to Sylvie, taking both her hands in his. "Don't you worry. Go back to your grandmother and tell her I'll be home late tonight. I'll go fetch Moses."

She hesitated for the briefest of moments, glancing at the assembled workers, then put her arms around him. "Be careful," she murmured. "I need both my lads back with me."

He grinned again and kissed her cheek. "We'll both come home safely. I promise."

Sylvie remained long enough to see Kit off, then practically ran home to let her grandparents know what had happened.

Supper was a quiet affair, though Sylvie noted the significant looks Grandmère was giving Grandpère. The looks continued into the evening as Sylvie took up her accustomed place on the sofa with her sewing, but couldn't seem to focus on the task.

"If Moses is on one of those wagons, he's not in danger," Grandpère said in a soothing tone. "Those animals will be treated like lords so they're in the best condition possible for sale."

"I know," Sylvie replied, putting her needle down. "But what if he's in with some of the larger animals? He could be trampled. Or sold before anyone can find him, and end up on someone's dinner table." She shuddered at the thought, then had another that was equally horrifying. "What if he isn't in any of the wagons at all?"

"Christopher will find your pet," Grandmère said with a sure smile. "He always comes through for you."

Kit did always come through for her. Every time she needed him, he was there to help, to comfort, to do everything he could to make the situation right.

"I hope I'm half as good a friend to him as he has been to me," Sylvie said, more to herself than anyone else.

Another hour passed and the sun began to set, raising Sylvie's anxiety level even further. Dark country roads were no place for a single rider with no lantern. It would be easy for his horse to misstep and injure itself or Kit.

"Ah, there he is, coming up the drive," Grandpère finally said after entirely too much time had passed.

Sylvie should have waited for Kit to take care of his horse, but she couldn't. Rushing out into the damp air, she picked up her skirts and ran into the barn. He was dismounting as she arrived, muddy and defeated.

She knew before he said the words that there would be no happy ending tonight.

"He wasn't in any of the wagons I checked," Kit said, wrapping his arms around her, "but there were two I couldn't get to before the light faded. They'll be at the market by now, and I can ride out tomorrow to see if he's there."

She kissed him then, heedless of who might see or know. He'd gone to great lengths to find a mere bird, for no other reason than said bird was important to her. "Thank you, Kit," she said softly, resting her cheek against his. "Thank you for trying."

Kit couldn't sleep that night thinking of how Sylvie's heart would break if Moses were lost to her. Every indication was that the goose was safely ensconced in a market stall with Kit's livestock, warm and comfortable for the night.

But what if something happened to him before Kit could get there?

As soon as the sky began to lighten, Kit washed and dressed, then headed to the barn to saddle his horse.

The ride to the Harvest Festival market was uneventful, even peaceful so early in the morning. But Kit urged his horse on, anxious to return the smile to Sylvie's beautiful face and, if he was totally honest, to see Moses himself unharmed. The bird had been something of a companion during the past two years, and had brought Kit and Sylvie together on many occasions.

One could even say Moses helped them fall in love.

Because Kit was certain now that he loved Sylvie. How could he not? She was kind and generous, not only with material items but with her time and her heart. She was practical and hard-working and lovely, and he didn't want to imagine his life without her.

Kit dismounted when he arrived at the market, walking his horse among the stalls as he looked for his livestock.

"Ah, there you are," he said aloud to them when he found the first group. "I've never been so happy to see a bunch of goats before."

He tied the horse to the corner post and began systematically searching the stalls containing his animals. But his heart sank a little more as each stall turned up chickens, goats, cows, and pigs but no goose.

"'Scuse me, mister, can I help you with something?" a man asked as Kit was leaning over the half-door of one stall examining the chickens within.

The man was dressed in work clothes, but wore a pencil behind his ear and carried what looked like a ledger. "Are these all the Mathison animals that were brought in last night?" The man looked askance at him, but Kit clarified, "I'm Christopher Mathison."

"Oh, yes, of course." The man flipped open the ledger, searching for the page he wanted, then tried to reconcile the information on the page with the animals in the stalls. Twice.

"No, it appears we're short." He went back to the ledger a third time, then nodded. "Oh, of course. The Duke of Alston's man was here yesterday afternoon when the first wagon came in. Apparently His Grace wants to add to his collection, and his man bought up that whole bunch."

"What?"

"Wanted to take possession of them immediately, and paid a pretty penny for them, too. Your man who came in with the animals authorized it, but wouldn't take the money with him when he left—we have it in the strongbox."

Well, that might come in handy. Because now he was going to have to ride thirty miles to retrieve a wayward goose.

Fortunately, the weather was clear for once and the roads were reasonably dry. Kit reached Orchard Lake, the Duke of Alston's home in Kent, by mid-afternoon. If all went well, there was time to find Moses, rest the horse, and still get back home to Sylvie before nightfall.

If all went well.

Kit was met by a groom who gave him directions and led his horse away to be cared for, then found himself standing before the great front door, suddenly conscious of his worn work clothes that smelled of the stables. But there was nothing he could do about it now.

A footman opened the door and left him to wait in the entryway when Kit asked for the steward.

"I must look like a beggar," he muttered, removing his hat and sliding a hand through his bristly hair.

"Not quite," a male voice answered crisply, "but the footman thought you were one of our tenant farmers."

Kit looked down at his frumpy tailcoat and the frayed cuffs of his trousers. "I can see why. Mathison is my name. You are the steward of this estate?"

"Jacobs," he said, shaking Kit's hand. "My office is this way."

Kit followed the steward through a series of hallways and into a darkly paneled room with little in the way of furniture, but floor to ceiling windows that let in much of the afternoon sun. He took the chair Jacobs offered him, and waited for the man to settle in his own seat behind the stout wooden desk.

"Now, what can I do for you, Mr. Mathison?"

"I'm here about a goose."

Jacobs gave him a quizzical look, and Kit told him about the transportation of his livestock to the market along with Moses's probable though mistaken inclusion.

"You came all the way from the Harvest Festival market for one goose?"

"Yes."

"Truly?"

Kit's chair was becoming uncomfortable, and he shifted slightly. "Yes. Do you have him or not?"

"Let me check the inventory." Jacobs stood, straightening his immaculate waistcoat and tailcoat, and walked slowly over to a table that held stacks of papers and what looked to be ledgers or account books. He selected one of the oversized ledgers, turned to the relevant page, then laid it on the table and began shuffling through a stack of papers.

And continued to shuffle.

Then went back to the ledger, ran his finger down the page, and returned to the stack of papers.

Was he being deliberately slow? Trying to impress the grandeur of the operation on Kit? It was difficult to believe he possessed any level of incompetence and still kept his position as the steward of a ducal estate.

After several more minutes of going back and forth, Jacobs located the item he was searching for and brought it back to his desk. "My apologies—we purchased several loads of livestock at the market yesterday. But yes, there was one white goose in the group of animals we purchased from C. Mathison."

Relief flooded his body, but his posture remained straight, his face—he hoped—expressionless. It could be the wrong goose, and even if it was the right one, Kit hadn't secured him yet. "Excellent. I will take him off your hands, with adequate compensation of course, and be on my way."

Jacobs smiled tightly. "Perhaps."

They negotiated for several minutes, but in the end Kit decided that Sylvie's happiness and Moses's safe return were worth more to him than time spent arguing over how much said goose was worth. "Ten percent over market value. That's far more than what you paid for him."

Jacobs hesitated, and Kit knew the man was toying with him.

"That's my final offer," Kit said, rising. "If you aren't interested, then our business is concluded."

He turned to leave, his heart in his throat, hoping that the steward didn't call his bluff and let him walk out the door with no bird.

"Ten percent over will do," Jacobs replied, a note of satisfaction creeping into his voice.

"Good. I'll see the bird first, then you'll get your money."

When they reached the barnyard, the steward spoke to one of the stable lads and stood to one side while work bustled on about him. "Bryant will fetch your goose."

Bryant was apparently much more efficient at his tasks than Jacobs, and returned with a ball of gleaming white feathers tucked under one arm.

"Moses?" Kit called.

The bird's head went up and his feet began flailing. Bryant shifted the goose against his chest and held on with both arms.

"Moses! There's the lad I'm looking for."

The flailing became whole-body thrashing accompanied by a series of excited honks.

"Satisfied?" Jacobs asked.

Kit grinned and reveled in the relief. "Yes. Very."

Chapter 7

IT HAD BEGUN TO DRIZZLE, but Sylvie sat outside under the big oak tree along the drive waiting for Kit to return. She dearly hoped that he would return with Moses, but knew that if he returned alone he'd have a plan to try again. As long as she'd known him, if Kit Mathison could solve a problem for someone he would do it.

It was a trait she'd come to cherish over the past several weeks. Not just because she benefited from it, but because he didn't do it for recognition or attention. He simply wanted to make her life easier because he cared about her.

Was there something she could do for him?

Shortly before sunset, a lone rider trotted up the drive and Sylvie jumped to her feet. "Kit?"

"We're home, lad," he said to the dark bundle tucked against him. A white head popped out and glanced around, then began honking.

"Moses!"

Kit handed down the bird, wrapped in a rough blanket, before he dismounted, and Sylvie hugged the bundle to her. After just a moment, Moses expressed his displeasure at being unceremoniously crushed and she unwrapped him, setting him loose to become reacquainted with his home.

Then she threw her arms around Kit.

"I don't know how you did it," she said softly, pressing a kiss to his wet cheek, his temple, "but I'm so glad you did."

He held her tightly, reciprocating each kiss she gave him. "I'll tell you the story later tonight, if you want to hear it. I'm sure your grandparents are anxious to have you back indoors, out of this rain."

The mention of her grandparents, who had a clear view of them from the sitting room, cooled her enthusiasm slightly, but she nodded. Whatever this was—or wasn't—between her and Kit, they did not need to play it out for an audience.

She did take his arm as they walked up the drive, and helped him stable his horse, unwilling to go inside until he was ready to do so. Moses came running into the barn behind them, honking happily with his wings spread, asking for neck scratches before darting back outside.

"Look how happy he is," Sylvie exclaimed, clasping her hands together. "Kit, I don't know how to thank you."

He stole one more kiss, murmuring, "We can talk about that later as well."

The butterflies returned to their fluttering in her stomach and she shivered deliciously. "Looking forward to it."

They somehow managed to go inside and eat supper with Sylvie's grandparents, then to sit side by side on the sofa in the sitting room afterward, as if they were two friends who were merely excited to have a special pet returned safely home.

Or at least, she thought they had. When Grandpère decided to go up to bed, Grandmère decided to follow but paused at the sofa. "Enjoy the evening," she said quietly, giving them a little wink.

Apparently they hadn't concealed their eagerness as well as she'd thought.

Well, no matter. The hour had finally arrived when Sylvie could thank Kit properly for bringing Moses back, and perhaps to figure out how she felt about this man who had, until very recently, been little more than an acquaintance to her these past two years.

She scooted closer to him on the sofa and took his hand in hers. "You must tell me how you managed to find Moses."

He gave her hand a squeeze, then explained his stop at the market, his negotiations with the steward at Orchard

Lake, and having to wrap Moses in the blanket in order to carry him on horseback.

"All that just to bring a bird back to me," she said when he finished.

Kit cleared his throat. "For you, yes."

His words squeezed her heart. "And I know that steward didn't just give you Moses. You will let me repay you for that cost at least."

"Absolutely not," he replied firmly.

She pressed her lips together for a moment. "I saw the roof yesterday, I know that it's nearly completed. You'll need to pay the builder very soon for everything you still owe him."

"You and your grandparents need every penny you can save," he reminded her. "I will have enough from the sale of my livestock to pay for the repairs to the house."

"Kit—"

"No," he said, turning to her, "I'll not budge on this point. If you feel that strongly about it you can owe me a favor, but I won't take your money."

She slid an arm around him and drew him down to her, capturing his lips with all the emotion she'd been suppressing. "You stubborn man," she mumbled, pulling back just a fraction of an inch before kissing him again.

His arms came around her, one big hand splayed across her back, holding her securely. "Yes, but you love me for it."

He was grinning, and likely joking, but her heart jumped into her throat and she rested her forehead against his. "I do love you, for your stubbornness and many other reasons."

"What?"

"I love you," she said softly, combing her fingers through his hair. "I can no longer pretend I don't."

Kit didn't pull away, but he didn't celebrate the news either. In fact, he didn't react at all. If it weren't for the increased thumping of his heart in his chest, Sylvie might have thought he hadn't heard her at all.

She loosened her arms about him. "I don't expect you to return my feelings—I've only just realized myself that I had them. But please don't say we can no longer be friends."

His eyes met hers in the light of her grandparents' treasured oil lamp and he traced a finger down her cheek. "I would never say that. You've caught me by surprise, that's all."

"You're sure?"

"Yes," he said with a nod. "I've also thought of a favor you can do for me, if you're willing."

"What's that?"

"Let me escort you to the Harvest Festival next week," he said. His voice was a bit rough and his breathing rapid, but his eyes were locked on hers.

Her hands found his shoulders. "That hardly seems like a fair trade after you rode half the county to bring Moses back to me."

"It's more than enough," he assured her. "Will you?"

His arms were still around her, his body warm against hers, and she wanted badly to kiss him again. But he'd spooked like a frightened horse when she told him she loved him, and she didn't want to spook him further.

Instead, she simply said, "It will be my pleasure."

The day before the Harvest Festival, Kit moved back into his own home. The repairs had been finished for several days, he'd hired a local woman to thoroughly clean the interior, and there was no longer any reason to continue staying with Sylvie and her grandparents.

He gathered his clothing and personal items together along with the loaves of bread Mrs. Devereaux had baked for him, and carried them to his house through a fine mist that emanated from low, dark clouds. Sylvie had offered to help him, but he'd declined. He wanted to get his head and his heart sorted out before spending time alone with her again, to decide what he wanted and what his next step should be. He had nearly burst with joy when she said she loved him, but no words would come when he'd attempted to summon them.

And now he was afraid he might well be too late.

Arriving at the house, Kit left the bread in the kitchen and headed up the stairs to the master's chamber. The last time he'd been there, water had poured from the ceiling and soaked everything within its reach. But when he opened the door, the room was freshly plastered and painted, the hole in the ceiling no longer even visible.

He put his things away, then sat down on the upholstered chair he kept by the large window and sighed.

"It cost me every penny I have, but I have my house back."

There were other problem areas the builder had identified which would need repairs sometime in the future, and the farm wasn't producing the way it had when Kit was a boy. He ought to sell it to someone with the means to restore it to its former glory, but despite the money and effort he knew he would be putting in—had already put in—he couldn't bring himself to do it.

Would Sylvie love this old heap as much as he did? Would she wish to preside over a home that was constantly in need of expensive repairs?

Did he want her to?

He had no doubt in the world that he loved Sylvie. He was less convinced that her declaration was true. Not that she would purposefully mislead him, of course, but he had returned her beloved pet to her thereby saving the goose from a fate as someone's Michaelmas dinner. Had she only thought she loved him because she was so relieved?

Or was she truly sincere?

Kit leaned his forehead against the cool glass and closed his eyes.

The memory of Sylvie in his arms overwhelmed him just then and his breath caught in his throat. Ye gods she was an amazing woman! What would it be like to wake up beside her every morning? To discuss the workings of the estate together, reinvigorate this house together, handle account ledgers together?

Handle account ledgers? If he thought that was romantic pastime, he *must* be in love.

What if she really did love him in return?

He stood and gave himself a mental shake. "I can't just sit here brooding all day. Even with the livestock sold and the crops ruined, there is still work to be done."

When Kit returned to the house later that evening, he was tired and sweaty, looking forward to washing, eating a quick supper, and going to bed early. But just as he was about to head upstairs, a knock sounded on the kitchen door. He trudged over and opened it, then rubbed his eyes. Had he conjured her with his thoughts?

"Good evening, Kit."

"Good evening, Sylvie." He opened the door wider and gestured for her to come inside, but couldn't help making a joke as she entered. "Miss me already?"

"Yes," she said with a grin. "But that's not why I'm here."

She touched his shoulder as she passed by him and his stomach did a somersault, then he cringed. He hadn't had a chance to wash or change yet, and he must smell like an ox.

But Sylvie didn't seem to notice or care. "I have a favor to ask of you."

"I'll do it."

She laughed lightly. "You don't even know what it is."

He took one of her hands and gave it a gentle squeeze. He didn't care what the favor was. He would do anything for this woman. Didn't she know that? "Very well then, what is your favor?"

"My grandparents' wedding anniversary is tomorrow, and I'd like to surprise them at the Harvest Festival. But I need a partner."

"Come sit down, and tell me what I'll need to do."

He led her into the sitting room, careful to choose an old, tatty chair for himself, pulling it closer to hers. She explained her plan, her eyes shining with excitement and love for her grandparents, and he couldn't help but love her more.

"I would be happy to," he said when she was finished. "And you're welcome to use the kitchen whenever is convenient. I'll be out most of the morning, but I'll leave the door open for you."

"Oh, Kit, thank you," she replied, clasping her hands together on one knee. "It's not much, but I think they'll enjoy it."

"I think so too." He paused, desperately wanting to tell her how much he loved her but unable to find the right words. Ah, but there was one thing he could do. "I'm glad you came over tonight, because I have something for you."

He excused himself and went to the room his mother used to jokingly call the conservatory because it was the sunniest room in the house. He returned with a slip of a plant in a small pot.

"It's not much to look at yet," he said, the slightest hint of trepidation creeping into his voice, "but I'm told that roses take some time to root properly from cuttings."

She stood and accepted the pot from him, curiosity written all over her face. "It's a rose cutting?"

He nodded, gaining confidence from her interest. "From the rose bush on the south side of the house. The variety is called 'Duchess of Portland.' My mama and papa planted it underneath the window of the master's chamber when they were first married. Apparently this variety was rather rare at the time, and neither of them would tell me how they happened to obtain one."

Her lovely eyes went wide. "What a wonderful way to celebrate their marriage. And you're giving me a cutting?"

"I took that cutting the day after our first kiss," he told her softly.

Her reaction was slightly delayed, as if it took her a moment to fully understand what he had said. Her gaze dropped to the nearly bare stem in the pot then back to Kit, her mouth forming a small o.

She set the pot on the floor, then stepped close to him and slid her arms around his neck, heedless of the sweat and smell. "Thank you," she whispered.

He closed his eyes and held her close against him, thankful that his gift could say what he couldn't.

Chapter 8

$\mathscr{S}$YLVIE TOOK KIT'S HAND AND climbed up into the old gig that he'd hauled out especially to drive her to the Harvest Festival. The day was overcast but dry for a change, so she'd planned to walk. But when Kit realized she'd be carrying the cake she'd baked in his kitchen earlier that day, he'd insisted on driving her. Grandmère and Grandpère had gone on ahead, smiling at her then at each other when she said she'd arrive with Kit a little later.

Kit clambered up onto the seat beside her, dressed in one of his finer tailcoats for the occasion, and took up the reins. "Ready?"

She nodded and the conveyance jerked into motion. Unfortunately, their conversation remained at a stand still. What did one say to the man who couldn't tell you he loved you in so many words, but did everything in his power to *show* you?

Nothing, apparently. But perhaps she could do a little showing of her own.

His hands were occupied driving and hers held the cake, but she slid closer to him on the seat so their arms and thighs were pressed lightly together. He glanced at her and grinned, and his body visibly relaxed.

When they arrived at the festival, Kit helped her down and kissed the back of her hand. "Go prepare and start letting people know. I'll see to the horse and find your grandparents."

She almost kissed him then, but now that they were in public they had to abide by the rules of propriety. Instead Sylvie squeezed his hand. "Excellent. I'll meet you near the musicians."

She skirted the festival grounds with her cake, covered with a kitchen towel to disguise its true contents, until she reached the area where a group of local musicians had arranged themselves. They had left room for dancing, though at the moment there were only a few small children bouncing around in approximate time to the music.

As promised, a small table had been placed there for her with a borrowed linen tablecloth folded atop it. She set the cake down carefully beside the table and spread the cloth across it, aligning each of the four embroidered clusters of wildflowers with the four corners of the table. The cake she placed at the center, but left it wrapped in its towel.

"What's all this, Miss Devereaux?"

Sylvie turned to see Mr. Norris, who lived just a few miles away from Broadstone, gesturing to the table. "This is a surprise for my grandparents—we're going to celebrate their golden wedding anniversary today."

"Oh, lovely! Can I do anything to help?"

"Yes," she said with a wide smile. "Can you help me spread the word? I'd like everyone to meet here. After the Duke of Alston makes his speech, we'll congratulate them and have some music. But my grandparents mustn't find out."

Mr. Norris gave her a little salute and headed off. Sylvie surveyed the table, gave the musicians a nod, then headed off herself to the flower sellers. The offerings were meager this year and her purse was light, but she managed to put together a modest bouquet of late-blooming pink peonies interspersed with stalks of dried lavender for her grandmother and a smaller peony for her grandfather's buttonhole.

"Aren't the flowers lovely, Mr. and Mrs. Devereaux?" came Kit's voice from some distance.

Sylvie turned hurriedly toward the sound and spotted him trying to steer Grandmère and Grandpère toward the animals. She flashed him a smile and darted in the opposite direction, talking the long way round to return to her cake, hoping she'd escaped unseen.

Finally, as the sun began to set, the Duke of Alston arrived in his grand carriage with his wife and son. He was the predominant landowner in this part of Kent, and he or one of his family had welcomed people to the Harvest Festival for as long as there had been one. Sylvie wondered momentarily at the man's health, as he needed to be helped from his carriage and was slowly escorted to the musicians' box by Her Grace and a sturdy footman.

The crowd began to gather around, and Sylvie searched the multitude of faces for Kit and her grandparents.

"There you are," came Grandpère's voice from behind her. "I was starting to suspect that Christopher was deliberately leading us away from you."

"Nonsense," Sylvie replied, trying to keep a straight face. "Why would he do that?"

"I don't know, but it certainly feels like he did."

Grandpère led Grandmère to one side of Sylvie, and Kit took up a position on her other side, brushing his fingers against hers.

His Grace made his welcome speech with a surprisingly strong voice, thanking everyone in attendance for all the hard work they put in this year even though the unusual weather had overwhelmed so many fields. He urged them to leave off their worries for one night and to enjoy the festival.

The assemblage applauded and Sylvie assumed the duke would take his leave, but he waited for the applause to die down and added one more thing. "I believe there is also a golden wedding anniversary to celebrate this night. Miss Devereaux? Are you ready?"

Sylvie's heart pounded and her eyes must have been as round as coins, but Kit's hand found hers and gave it a reassuring squeeze. "How's that for an introduction?" he whispered.

She squeezed back and made her way through the crowd, curtsying before the duke and allowing him to bow over her hand. "Thank you, Your Grace."

"Tell your grandparents I hope they have many more happy years together."

"I will."

The duke gestured for the duchess and footman, and allowed himself to be escorted away. Sylvie stood watching him for a long moment, wondering how on earth he'd found out about the anniversary.

Taking a deep breath, she turned to the festival goers and smiled brightly. "His Grace is correct—my grandparents, Monsieur and Madame Devereaux, are celebrating their fiftieth wedding anniversary today. I hope you'll join me in congratulating them on so many wonderful years together."

Kit parted the crowd for her grandparents, gesturing for them to stand beside her near the musicians' box. Sylvie presented them with the flowers and unveiled the cake, brimming over with happiness for the two people that had raised her.

"One more thing," she said, looking to the musicians and giving them a nod. "Will you lead off the dancing?"

They looked at each other as the musicians tuned their instruments.

"Will you do me the honor?" Grandpère asked, offering her his hand.

Grandmère grinned. "It will be my pleasure."

Other couples joined in when the music began, but Sylvie hung back to just watch them enjoying the moment.

Kit found her, slipping an arm around her. "They look like they're having fun."

She leaned against him and sighed. "Good. That was the plan."

"Would you like to dance?" he asked softly.

She took his hand in both of hers and drew his arm more securely around her waist. "I'd rather stay here," she replied. "With you."

Such an intimate pose was highly improper in public, but Sylvie didn't care. For once she was going to do what the Duke of Alston had suggested—forget her worries and enjoy the evening.

The last note of music died away in the moonlight, and the dancers began to go their separate ways. Kit sat off to one side watching them. Some left as soon as the music stopped, some took a moment to say their goodbyes, and some lingered together as if they were reluctant to part.

Sylvie had been dancing with her grandfather, laughing through the steps of a country dance that neither of them executed very well. When the music ended, they bowed and curtsied to each other, and Kit expected Mr. Devereaux to escort his granddaughter away. But instead, Sylvie came to Kit.

Alone.

"That turned out rather well, don't you think?" she asked when she reached him.

"The festival or your grandparents' anniversary?"

"Both." She sat down close beside him but didn't touch him. "Did you enjoy yourself?"

He nodded, aching to have her in his arms again but electing to remain still for the time being. "I did. I wasn't sure I wanted to come this year, but I'm glad I did."

Her gaze met his as the last of the clouds drifted away revealing a sky full of dainty, twinkling stars, and for the briefest of moments he thought she might kiss him. When she didn't, the disappointment nearly overwhelmed him.

"Are you returning home with your grandparents?" he asked.

"I think they could use some time to themselves," she responded, her smile softening. "Would you mind driving me?"

"Not at all. Shall we sit here for a while and let them get a head start?"

Sylvie twined her arm around his. "That's just what I was thinking.

Kit's heart began to pound as hard as the hammers that the builder's men had swung during his roof repair. "Good. There's actually something I'd like to speak to you about, and I think it will be easier to do if neither of us is focused on directing a pair of half-ton animals."

"Oh?"

He glanced around, noting the only people still nearby were the musicians packing up their instruments. A handful of other festival goers remained, but they were attending their own affairs. "A few days ago, you told me that you loved me."

The big full moon was bright overhead, and Sylvie's deep blush was evident. "Kit—"

"To my everlasting shame, I didn't say it back to you then," he continued, covering her hand with his. "I wanted to, and I'm still not sure why the words would not come. Because, Sylvie, I do love you."

"You do?"

Her eyebrows were raised, her head tilted slightly and he chuckled. "I would be skeptical, too, if I were you."

"No, it isn't that I don't believe you." She slid her hand down his arm and laced her fingers with his. "In fact, I know you love me. I just didn't expect you to say it."

"What do you mean you know?"

She grinned, and laid her head on his shoulder. "I knew for certain when you went to find Moses. You're a kind man, but that was more than even you would do for most people."

Kit thought back to those two days, searching wagon-loads of smelly animals crowded together, bargaining with that smug steward. "I absolutely would have done the same thing for Thomas or my mother. Maddie, too." He kissed the top of her head. "I didn't think twice about doing it for you, either."

She nodded. "I thought that when I told you I loved you that night, you'd return the sentiment. When you didn't, I suspected you either needed more time or you just weren't a man that expressed his emotions in words."

"Well, you were right," he murmured against her hair. "I needed time. I wasn't sure you were actually in love with me or just grateful I brought Moses back."

She straightened and met his eyes. "Oh, I hadn't even considered that."

"But when I gave you that rose cutting..."

Her expression turned dreamy and her body softened. "Any doubts I might have had about your feelings for me were put to rest right then."

The grounds were nearly deserted now. He released her hand and slid his arm around her, drawing her even closer to him. "Good," he said, his voice gruff with emotion. "That's what I had intended."

They sat together in the moonlight for several minutes, relaxing against each other. But all too soon, Sylvie sat up and turned to face him.

"There is something else I wanted to ask you about."

"What's that?"

"A few weeks ago, you proposed marriage to me." She clasped his free hand in hers and dropped her gaze to her lap as if to gather her courage, before meeting his eyes once again. "Is that offer still available?"

Kit shook his head, but couldn't keep the grin from his face. "That proposition was for a marriage of convenience. We were going to pool our resources to pay the rent on Broadstone and repair my house, remember?"

She searched his eyes, and her grin matched his. "Then let me make you a better one. I propose a marriage based on love and partnership and trust."

"We may have to work on our communication skills a bit more," he laughed, the joy of the moment breaking over him in the most delightful waves.

"I agree," she replied, her grin widening, "So I'll be plain. I love you, Kit Mathison, and I would very much like to have you as my husband."

"I love you, Sylvie Devereaux, and I would be honored to be your husband. Will you be my wife?"

The words had rushed out of him as if they were trying to escape, not in the measured manner he had tried for. But it didn't matter. Sylvie's arms came around him and her lips brushed his ear as she whispered her answer.

"Yes."

Chapter 9

YLVIE'S HEART WAS SOARING AS her betrothed handed her into the gig for the trip home. But there was one nagging voice in the back of her mind that kept asking questions she couldn't answer.

Would her grandparents be able to take care of the farm without her?

Could they pay the quarterly rent without the money she was earning?

Would her parents finally return to England to care for her grandparents when Sylvie went to live with Kit?

Kit was driving with both hands, but one arm was entwined with Sylvie's and she held it tightly.

"What's wrong?" he asked.

"How do you know something's wrong?" she countered, trying to make her voice light.

He bent his head toward hers. "Your fingernails are going to leave marks in my arm through my coat."

Sylvie immediately loosened her grip. "I'm sorry. I'm just worried about the effect this marriage will have on us and our families."

"It's time for practicalities, then," he said, pressing a kiss to her temple, then straightening to watch the road. "Very well. What is your biggest worry?"

"My grandparents," she said without hesitation. She listed off her questions regarding their welfare and was surprised when he smiled.

"We can't predict what your parents might do, but once we're wed you'll only be next door. And so will I. We can work out how to ensure your grandparents won't be overwhelmed by work."

He said it in such a matter-of-fact way that her heart rate slowed almost to normal. "It's that easy?"

"That part is." He pressed his lips together, squinting at the small patch of road that was illuminated by the lamps hanging from either side of the gig. "My estate is not in the same financial health that it was when I offered for you the first time, but we can sit down with your grandparents and sort things out together. Pool our resources, even if it's not exactly how I'd originally planned."

A measure of relief flowed through her. She expected no less from this man than to care about the people important to her, else she wouldn't be marrying him. But it still felt good to hear the words aloud. "That's an excellent idea."

The questions in her mind didn't vanish, but they quieted enough that Sylvie could enjoy the rest of the drive. They decided to go to Kit's home first to unhitch the horses and put them to bed, then took the lanterns from the gig and walked the familiar path to Broadstone Farm.

As they approached the house, Sylvie became jittery, fairly bouncing up to the door.

"Nervous?" Kit asked, taking her hand and giving it a reassuring squeeze.

She squeezed back and grinned broadly. "Excited. They love you almost as much as I do, and I'm looking forward to telling them that you'll be their grandson by marriage."

They entered the house and found Grandmère and Grandpère in their usual places in front of the fire.

"We've returned," Sylvie said brightly as they came into the sitting room, "and we have news."

Grandpère was holding a small damask bag in his lap. "So do we." He eyed their clasped hands and grinned. "Let us tell our news first. Then we can spend the rest of the evening celebrating yours."

Sylvie's face warmed but Kit was standing tall, his chest puffed out proudly. "Certainly. What is your news?" she asked.

"We received an anniversary gift from the Duke of Alston," Grandpère told her, handing her the damask bag.

Sylvie released Kit's hand and took the bag, pulling open the draw strings. "These are gold guineas."

"Five of them," Grandmère chimed in. "One for each decade we have been married, the card said."

"Five guineas?" Sylvie repeated incredulously.

"Not enough to get us through a winter with no crops," Grandpère clarified, trying —and failing—to maintain a serious expression, "but between those, the sale of your animals, and our savings, we'll be able to pay the rent and have money left over."

"That's wonderful!" Sylvie exclaimed. "Kit, do you know what this means?"

Kit grinned broadly. "We can be married as soon as the banns are called?"

Grandmère sat up straighter in her chair. "Married?"

Sylvie looked to Kit then nodded, unable to keep the smile from returning to her face.

Grandmère jumped up from her chair and enveloped Sylvie in a warm embrace. "Oh, my sweet Sylvie, I'm so happy for you!"

Grandpère rose, too, and put an arm around Kit's shoulders. "I hope you have as many happy years together as we have."

Grandmère embraced Kit as well, jubilant tears in her eyes. "Oh yes! If you are as happy together as we have been, what a marvelous life you will have together."

After another round of hugs, they sat before the fire and made plans for a wedding later that autumn when the leaves would be deep oranges and reds. Kit wrote a letter to his mother and one to his brother, promising to keep them informed of the exact date when it was chosen.

But soon enough, Grandmère and Grandpère gave each other a knowing look and declared they were tired.

"You may stay for another hour, Christopher," Grandpère told him. "Anything left unsaid after that will have to wait until tomorrow."

"We will expect you for breakfast, though," Grandmère said cheerily. "And for supper, too."

Kit accepted both invitations, and Sylvie's grandparents went up to bed. Then at last, Sylvie was alone with her betrothed. The long day was wearing on her, but there was one thing she wanted to do before attempting to sleep.

"Kit," she said, wrapping her arms around his waist, "may I kiss you?"

"I wish you would," he murmured, sliding his arms around her shoulders.

She had to reach a bit, but she captured his lips once, twice, then slid her hands down to cup his backside as she kissed him a third time.

He drew back a fraction of an inch and grinned. "You remembered."

"I did," she said, matching his grin. "I want to learn all the contours of your body...and your heart."

"You know the contours of my heart already," he replied softly, caressing her cheek. "Tonight, when you said yes, I realized you've held my heart for far longer than I knew."

Her throat closed with emotion, and this time it was Sylvie who couldn't answer in words. Instead, she slid her arms around him and pulled him tightly against her, sighing with a contentment she didn't know was possible when he reciprocated.

"I love you," she managed to whisper.

"I love you, too," he whispered back.

Ready for more Maitland Maidens?
Turn the page to read the first chapter of

Save the Last Dance for Me

Maitland Maidens Book 1

Chapter 1

April 1813

Benedict had literally backed himself into a corner.

He felt the ballroom wall bump solidly against his shoulder and discovered he was more than a little relieved. At least no one could ambush him from behind.

No one was approaching from the front, though, either. Here he was with hundreds of people at the first great entertainment of the Season, and even the chaperones and spinsters wanted little to do with him.

Not that he blamed them. Most of the *ton* had heard the details of Whitby's Christmas house party by now. They'd know how tongue-tied and awkward Benedict had been, even with the maids when he'd had occasion to speak to one. They'd know how his face had gone distinctly red whenever his turn came at charades, and how he'd inadvertently insulted Whitby's neighbor with what turned out to be a very politically charged remark. Everyone who cared to listen to the gossip would know that he'd given up after that, and spent the remainder of the party in the library, hiding away where he could neither inflict nor receive further harm.

Not that his cowardice had put Lady Whitby off. She'd been upset, of course. But here in her own ballroom with the crème of the *beau monde* swirling all around her, Lady Whitby was in her element. In fact, she was more determined than ever to find him a suitable wife, making lists of eligible young widows and new debutantes, practically following him around Town as he attempted to go about his business.

And she'd just spotted him.

He watched with a sort of detached fascination as she homed in on him from across the room like a hound after a stag. Even amid the bustle and noise of the crowd, the music of the orchestra, and the myriad of people stopping to speak with her, she remained focused on Benedict. Perhaps if he stayed completely still—

"Oh!" a female voice cried. A weight came down on his foot as the rustle of fabric swept against his legs. His arms reached out instinctively and caught hold of a soft form in a white gown dotted with silver embroidery.

"Thank you, sir," the voice said, a little breathless as its owner attempted to right herself. One pale hand braced itself against the lapel of his black evening coat while the other found his shoulder. A curl of dark hair brushed against his cheek. "My dance partner seems rather too vigorous this evening."

"Honoria?"

Long-lashed lids lifted to reveal a pair of eyes as dark as her hair, and her mouth curved into a surprised smile. "Benedict! I didn't know you'd be here tonight."

Aware that heads were turning their way, he removed his arms from her waist and clasped her hands in his, extracting them from his body with as much subtlety as he could manage.

"Isn't everybody here?"

Her gloved hands slipped from his and he felt a pang of regret. Once upon a time a reunion between the two of them would have included a warm—and deliberate—embrace. They were in public, though, and whatever their relationship had previously been, he reminded himself that it would hardly be the same after his years spent abroad.

Her gaze dropped to his waistcoat—silver silk with little leaves embroidered on it, made especially for this ball—and she smoothed her hands over her skirt, making the silver threads catch the light from the chandeliers above. "No one would miss the marchioness's Black and White Ball, of course. But you were never one for society affairs." Her eyes shifted back to his. "Is that why you're over here in the corner? Do you think to hide from the revelry rather than participate in it?"

Well, at least her directness hadn't changed. "As it happened, you're lucky I was here in this particular corner. If I had been out among the revelers, you would have fallen."

Honoria glanced around and Benedict followed suit, noting that people had turned back to their previous activities—except for Lady Whitby. She had resumed her course and was headed directly for him.

"Then for once I appreciate your wallflower ways." She grinned up at him. "You have saved me from what surely would have been the *on dit* of the week."

"Judging by what I saw on the terrace earlier, you would not have even been the *on dit* of the evening. But you could repay an act of gallantry with one of your own."

"What would you have me do?"

He took her hand and laid it on his sleeve. "Walk with me and pretend you enjoy my company."

Lady Honoria Maitland strolled through the ballroom beside her old friend, hoping this was the turning point she'd been waiting for all evening. She'd run into one aggravation after another since the moment she arrived. The shawl she'd worn against the chilly spring night had caught on the door latch of the carriage and torn. Her stepmother had introduced her to two gentlemen whose acquaintance she had previously made but desperately wished she hadn't. She'd accepted a third gentleman's request for a dance hoping to escape the first two, and nearly ended up face down on the floor.

But then Benedict Grey had caught her, and the evening began to show some promise. It had been months and months since they'd even seen each other, and so much longer since they'd had a real conversation. Perhaps that could be remedied tonight.

"Of course I will walk with you. Perhaps we can evade my dance partner—I have no desire to return to his ministrations. And I always enjoy your company."

They strolled away from his corner refuge with all the dignity of visiting royalty. Or at least Honoria did—spine straight, shoulders back, chin up. Benedict's eyes darted around the room as if he was plotting his escape.

Perhaps he was.

But his voice was calm when he spoke again. "Where shall we walk?"

"Let's take a turn about the room for a start." She grinned. "Because if the activities you witnessed on the terrace are still in progress, we'll want to avoid going there."

Benedict merely nodded, so she wracked her brain for another option and decided that a little forwardness would not go amiss with this man. At least, it never had before. "Dancing is also a good way to occupy one's time at a ball."

He cringed visibly. "You want to dance?"

"I love to dance, you know that." Her mouth and feet both paused while she looked more closely at her friend. His shoulders were slightly hunched as he halted beside her, and she could just make out a red tint creeping into his cheeks from beneath his snow white cravat. "Or, you used to know that. Have you forgotten all those afternoons we practiced together when we were young?"

"The afternoons I remember well." He took a half step closer to her and bent his head toward hers. "It's the steps I've forgotten."

"Truly?"

Benedict's eyes trailed down toward his shoes. "Yes, well, there isn't much call for a reel or a quadrille in the middle of an ancient ruin, is there?"

"I suppose not. "Honoria's mouth curved into a slow smile as an idea popped into her head. "But if you're in Town to stay, you'll need to re-acquire that skill."

She must have looked more mischievous than she realized because he straightened abruptly. "You sound like Lady Whitby."

"Is she the one you were hiding from?"

"I was *not* hiding."

The couple nearest them turned for a moment, and Honoria offered what she hoped was an apologetic look before tugging Benedict into motion. "Very well, you weren't hiding. But is the lady in question acting...rather too zealously for your taste?"

"That would be the most polite way to describe her efforts, yes." They walked along without speaking for a few paces before Benedict inched closer again. "What do you know about it?"

Honoria patted his sleeve. "I know only what news your mother has passed along to my stepmother, and that mainly consisted of your continued health and bachelorhood."

His gaze snapped to hers as if he'd been startled by her words. When he coughed and forced a smile, she knew she'd caught him out.

"Ah, so that's what Lady Whitby is after. She wants to see you wed."

"'To a woman of good breeding, with a pretty face and a head for details'," he quoted in an unnaturally high voice. He cleared his throat and resumed his own tenor. "The succession must be secured, of course."

Honoria grimaced, her gaze drifting toward the people in front of them. "A familiar tale in my home as well. 'You're eight-and-twenty, Honoria. If you weren't a duke's daughter no gentleman would even give you the time of day'."

"Is eight-and-twenty really so old?"

She glanced up at the rather plaintive note in his voice, recalling too late that he was the same age. "It is for a woman. It's ancient for an unmarried woman."

"Then why haven't you married?"

An impertinent question if there ever was one. And one that she was not prepared to discuss in the middle of a grand ball.

"We were talking about you." She spied a set of open French windows ahead and inclined her head toward them. "Why don't we go out onto the terrace after all...that is, if there are no longer indecent acts being performed out there. I may have an idea that will help you, and we'll want a little privacy to talk."

He studied her face for a long moment, then nodded once and led her out into the night. The darkness was tempered by torches lit at regular intervals along the balustrade and a gibbous moon rising over the horizon.

Beside her Benedict breathed deeply in, exhaling with a gentle "Ah."

The cool air felt wonderful on Honoria's heated skin. But rather than say so she took the opportunity to tease him a little. "Too much for you in there?"

"I'd forgotten what a ballroom full of people *smelled* like. So many bodies crowded together, and every single one of them wearing some sort of fragrance. It's...oppressive. It pushes down upon one until the body can bear it no more."

They found a stone bench to one side and Honoria sat, arranging her skirts about her. "You miss Greece, don't you?"

He settled down next to her, his posture relaxing. "I do. But I didn't mean to be so vulgar about it. Please accept my apologies."

"There is no need to apologize to me for speaking frankly. You've said worse than that in my hearing, and I'm quite sure I have in yours. Or have you forgotten the time we 'liberated' that bottle of wine when we were fifteen?"

"I remember it well. You drank half of it before I could get through a glassful—"

"I did no such thing!"

"—and the next day you proceeded to describe to me in great detail just how very vile you felt."

He was laughing now, not a polite chuckle but a sound of genuine amusement. Honoria felt herself laughing along with him. "And you did the same. If memory serves, you even told me how many times you cast up your accounts."

His eyes rolled skyward. "Promise me you won't tell Lady Whitby that story. I would never hear the end of her etiquette lessons."

Honoria turned toward him, searching his face in the low light. "Has she been that meddlesome, then?"

Benedict shook his head, meeting her gaze as his mouth drew down into a more sober expression. "No. Well yes, she has, but I am trying not to mind—she simply has a vested interested in my future nuptials and wants to ensure they take place."

"Will you tell me about it?"

Honoria held her breath for a moment and waited. They used to tell each other everything, but when Benedict had put actual distance between them by sailing away to the Continent, an emotional distance had been created as well. It was one thing to share a fond memory, but what of the present?

His brows crowded together, the way they had when he'd thought intensely about something as a younger man. "She is the wife of a peer, and has given him no son to inherit. Nor likely will she."

"And so she's turned to matchmaking for you."

Her voice was soft and, when Benedict didn't respond, she thought perhaps he hadn't heard her. But then he nodded, bowing his head slightly. "She has."

"For her good, if not yours." Honoria grasped the stone bench with both her hands. "Well, I did say that I had an idea for you."

He straightened, his hair catching the torchlight—it had lightened considerably during his years away to a soft sandy brown. "I'm listening."

"You need to find a wife."

"Yes."

"But you can't dance."

His large hands clapped down over his knees. "What does one thing have to do with the other?"

Honoria put on the air of patient authority she used when conversing with her eight-year-old half-brother. "You must dance with a lady in order to court her. How else will you determine if you can even stand her company?"

"Can I not talk to her?"

Honoria shook her head, setting the ringlets on either side of her face to swaying. "Talking is not enough. One only discovers a person's true character when one speaks with that person alone. But when does a gentleman have the opportunity to speak alone with a lady?"

"We're alone now."

She looked for the twitching of his lips or crinkling of his eyes to suggest he was being facetious, but his serious expression remained fixed.

"We are. But how much longer will that last, do you think? How long before my stepmother begins to look for me?" Her fingers clenched the bench seat with more force. "And what would happen to my reputation if we were found together out here?"

"I see your point."

"Dancing accomplishes so much more. There is time for talking, of course, but there is also a chance to flirt, and to touch. One can study a partner's appearance without being rude or vulgar, and discover if said partner is graceful or clumsy or featherbrained or bookish."

Benedict sighed. "It's a necessity, then."

"Yes. And I will teach you."

"You?"

She tilted her head slightly to the side. "Me. Or you'll have to hire a dancing master."

She watched his fingers tense on his knees as he digested that bit of information. But he didn't reply.

A light breeze rustled the flowers in the garden nearby. The torch flames flickered, casting peculiar shadows across the terrace. Then all was still once more—including Benedict. She waited for several more minutes but he remained silent.

"Think it over, why don't you?" Honoria rose from the bench and smoothed the fine cambric of her gown. "Take me driving tomorrow, and we can discuss it further if you like."

Benedict stood and offered her his arm. "I'll call for you at four."

He fell quiet again escorting her back into the house, and she wondered if she'd offended him. No one liked to dwell on his own deficiencies, certainly. But the Benedict she knew six years ago would have teased her in return about a shortcoming of her own.

Clearly, he was no longer the man he'd once been.

"Honoria?"

She blinked herself out of her musings. "Yes?"

"I would marry you, you know."

She froze. "What?"

"If we were caught together. If I compromised you." His eyes met hers in the half-light. "And not just because I'm looking for a wife now. I would have then, too."

He didn't have to explain when *then* was. She knew he was thinking of the day her mother died. He never did tell her how he'd gained entry into the house or how he found her bedchamber without disturbing anyone, but he'd managed to do both late that night. He'd sat with her and held her hand as she had talked of her mother, then cradled her against him when she'd wept. Only when she had calmed did either of them realize the potential for an immense scandal his presence caused. And even then he'd stayed with her until she fell asleep.

Her fingers tightened on his sleeve in response. Perhaps some of the old Benedict still existed after all.

Other Books by Cora Lee

Sweet & Traditional:
Save the Last Dance for Me (Maitland Maidens #1)
Back In My Arms Again (Maitland Maidens #2)
Kissing by the Mistletoe (Maitland Maidens #3)
A Kiss to Build a Dream On (Maitland Maidens #4)
When I Fall In Love (Maitland Maidens #5)

Spicy Novellas:
What If I Loved You

Spicy and Suspenseful:
No Rest for the Wicked
The Good, The Bad, And The Scandalous
The Duke of Darkness

About The Author

Cora Lee is National Bestselling author of Regency romance. She went on a twelve year expedition through the blackboard jungle as a high school math teacher before publishing *Save the Last Dance for Me*, the first book in the Maitland Maidens series. She then followed it up with six more novels and novellas, ranging from sweet and traditional to spicy and suspenseful.

When she's not walking Rotten Row at the fashionable hour or attending the entertainments of the Season, you might find her participating in Regency Fiction Writers events, wading through her towering TBR pile, or eagerly awaiting the next Marvel movie release. If you'd like to find out more about Cora or her books you can visit her website, sign up for her newsletter, or connect with her on Bookbub, Facebook, or Goodreads.